Giving Up Architecture

ELIZA MOOD

Published by Seaglass Books
Meirion House
Glan yr afon
Tanygrisiau
Blaenau Ffestiniog
Gwynedd LL41 3SU
www.seaglassbooks.co.uk

The right of Eliza Mood to be identified as author of this work has been asserted by her in accordance with the Copyright, Designs and Patent Act, 1988. © 2006 Eliza Mood

ISBN 0-9549433-9-2

British Library Cataloguing in Publication Data. A CIP record for this book can be obtained from the British Library

Designed and typeset in Garamond by Seaglass Books

Cover from an original painting by Colin Moss © Colin Moss www.colinmossstudio.com & adapted from a photograph of the original artwork by Lucy Sclater www.sclater.co.uk

Acknowledgements

In writing this book I benefited immeasurably from the perceptive advice of 'The Escape Committee': Carole Coates and Rita Ray. Also from the supportive critical comments of Maggie Mood, John Coates, Vick Lawless, Keith Maiden, Bryan Hopkinson, Fiona Frank, Mick Murphy and Faye Simpson. I am indebted to my publisher, Jan Fortune-Wood of Seaglass Books, for intelligent and incisive editing. Information on the period, planes, and bulls was generously given by Pat Cardy, Eric Holden, David Wood and Tony Birkett.

Eliza Mood is a lecturer in English Language and writes on storytelling and narrative. She is a member of 'Sixpoets' and has had several poems published. *Giving Up Architecture* is her first novel. Her author website can be found at: www.elizamood.co.uk

Giving Up Architecture

*For Robert Mood (1925-2000), present in thought,
and to Maggie Mood, wonderful storyteller.*

Autumn Term, 1949

The Man who had no story to tell

Prologue

Clem

Clem's mind shifted gear. He rose from his body and viewed the room, himself in the centre, supine and with a hole in his sock. He travelled upward, out of his room and over a great distance, across a sea and hills until below him lay interlocking tessellations of roofs, points of spires and domes of a city. As he moved closer, buildings shivered and slumped as though a course of stones had been removed from the foot of each. Windows rattled and cracked. Floors groaned and collapsed into dust which flew upward and darkened the air. Clouds formed momentarily into schlosses and palaces, pyramidal structures, domes, arches and balconies. Through the dust he glimpsed stepped gables and steeply inclined roofs, baroque elevations with curvilinear outlines, classical features grafted onto gothic structures.

Hybrids fractured, facades were dismantled, terminals, scrollwork and obelisks toppled. His eyes were blinded by dust. Dust filled him. Hidden

9

sea creatures, ferns and shells that had once imprinted the inner sands of buildings were crushed into particles and exposed, drifting as dust before settling as a layer of sand coating the cities of Europe, dry as drifts in a desert.

There were muffled bumps and banging as he tried to gather himself together. He was lying in a grey place covered with grey dust. It littered his hair and smeared out the light from his eyes. He was immobilised by a mire of fallen masonry. It was safer to avoid ending up in these places he had sworn never to revisit.

September

Lou

"But how can you know?" Lou laid the photograph on the table and squinted at Fern. Her friend looked smaller and paler than usual. "You still have four months to go... or is it... because of the way it was conceived –" There were so many things she wanted to say, but she drew back; the way she had as a child on the shore when her foot almost crushed a clutch of oyster catcher eggs in a scrape of pebbles.

"It's just a feeling," said Fern stroking where the limpet was growing inside, "That something isn't....quite right."
Inside, Lou guessed, Fern was shaking.
"Maybe the terror of it –"
"Of *rape*?"
Lou knelt by her. "You are still *you*...Fern."

"I don't know Lou. I don't feel like me any more... not just because of the limpet." She brought her knees up. "I suppose if I'd chosen this, then the father would be part of me...." She frowned. "There's supposed to be cyanide in the seed of ferns." After a moment she continued, "Let me see it anyway." She reached for the photograph.

The crinkled sepia image was taken only seven years ago, thought Lou, but already she couldn't decipher their expressions. Minutes before, her father in one of his lighter humours had sprung across the pier boards still clutching his concertina. The band huddling on the promenade blew their cornets fit to wake the dead. On the beach below were barbed wire and notices to stay clear in case of unexploded bombs. Surprising that the photographer and his *Brownie Box* had been there at all that day.

Her father waved them on as they raced over a strip of uncordoned beach towards him, laughing between trying to catch their breath. And then the flash. Fern's pigtails blurred as they swung and her lips parted to speak... On the back was a pencil scribble in her father's hand. 'Day after *Möhne* Dam, May 17th, 1943'.

Fern stood and crossed to the window and Lou noticed the rounding was perceptible. Another demobbed soldier who couldn't settle; sent off the rails by war. At the trial he had testified that a voice told him to do it. Mother gave Fern refuge in the attic bedroom when Vera refused to have her daughter back. And all the while Lou was far away at St. Hild's in Durham.

Lou glanced back at the photograph. Those days on the shore when they dallied along the firmer sand among razor shells, shrapnel, fishing line, the bits of net tangled with great hanks of hair-like stuff and slimy, dark-green eel weed were another life now. The days when they had planned how they would be free of war were receding like the tide.

That day, as every day, they would have been telling stories in the slippage between one tide and the next, trudging in their lace up shoes, their overlong hand-me-down overcoats trailing...

...arms linked, Fern elegant in cast-offs with the sleeves rolled up. Oyster catchers called and ringed plovers flitted ahead of them over the pebbly patch. Back in the adult world their mothers were preoccupied with queuing and caring for second cousins who turned up with nowhere else to go. No-one had time to keep a watchful eye on girls who said their prayers and spent Sunday at meeting. They staved off the moment of return to the world of blackout cloth and saying grace over the rations on the Morrison shelter top, ignoring the chill as the sun's warmth ebbed from the sand. Fern flipped her thick black plaits free of her overcoat and shook her head; even in the wind she was hatless. Lou pulled up her collar and

13

shrugged down deeper into the coat, her brown school beret cocked to one side.

Wind whipped the backs of the dunes and spat bitter wasps of sand around their shins. This place was borrowed from the sea; a place to skim stones into the foam before the next bomb dropped. But even here the wireless voices could sometimes invade. Last night it was the *Möhne* Dam. Someone had invented bombs that skipped over the water, then sank and exploded under the surface bursting a dam and forming a tidal wave that would 'carry all before it'. The voice sounded like a preacher on *Revelations*, "The sheer force and power of water will carry all before it." The thought of drowning had flashed through Lou's mind; how easily your wick might be snuffed. She stopped short. "I refuse to be suffocated in a gas mask and if I live to have children, I swear I'll never make them wear one." She blinked away the thought of gas drill at school.

"Even to save their lives?" asked Fern.

Lou turned and sat on the edge of the table of rock, "What world is worth living in if someone is forever trying to put out your light?"

Fern wormed the toe of her boot into the soft muddy silt. After a while she asked, "What did you think of the thing Miss Spark said before *Precious Bane* the other day?" She crouched to inspect a child's spinning top, rusted and half-buried in the muddy sand.

14

"You mean about how we must read as many books as we can so that we have them under our belts and are armed for better times to come?"

When they walked out onto the mud the smell was not salt but subtler; bleach or ammonia or perhaps some gas which could send you to sleep, thought Lou. Their lives were slipping away like gas into air.

"Yes and not to rush into marriage and let our lives slip by in unending days of soaping collars and cuffs,"

"Mmm." Lou thought about the young men she had known; older boys they had idolised, like Stephen Berard whose parents were also officers in the Mission and who had come to her father for advice about his poetry. If men like Stephen were dying in the mud what hope was there for her or Fern?

"If we weren't growing up in the middle of a war perhaps we could believe in the future more easily."

The tide was coming in; waters sculpting the sand into ridges. They retraced their steps, making for home as thistle seeds blew over the pasture by the sea...

...sea now glimpsed at a distance through the rooftops from her room at the top of the house. Now that she was beginning a new life the memories returned more vividly and regularly. It was five years ago that the family moved to an upstairs flat and attic; evicted from their home on Herne Hill in the Mission's attempt to avoid scandal. It still hurt that even *they* didn't believe her father. Now he was dying of coronary thrombosis and a troubled spirit.

The doctors called it oversensitivity, poor nerves, but Lou blamed the war and... the other thing... It had begun with the guilt of being at home when his friends were in the trenches. Even today she wondered what had held him back, why he hadn't ministered to the troops during the war. She didn't like to ask questions, but one day she would vindicate her father.

In the attic bedroom she shared with Fern, Lou fumbled for the notebook in the back of the desk drawer. Something rolled about and she felt for it, warm and smooth to the touch; the old piece of amber.

She opened the exercise book at the page she had used earlier, 'Lesson Three: Poetry'. She would be a teacher, after all, not an actress trained at the Royal Academy of Dramatic Art or the Rose Bruford to be opened next year. It was what her father wanted and he was dying.

Class 2C was difficult, the other teachers told her. Doctor Barnardo's was full to overflowing with war orphans or children of fathers who never came back, one too many for the mother who relied on family or the new welfare. They had been snatched from their cots to the lullaby of grumbling planes, rocked to sleep in shelters to the sounds of shattering glass and dreams; the unteachable ones. Perhaps she might show them wind dispersal of seeds using dandelion clocks as she had done as a trainee. Lou was glad she had been at Hild's, but the war had blown them all off course. Back in the storytelling days neither she nor Fern imagined they might find themselves here. Sometimes it was hard to believe that her friend was the same Fern, the one who had balanced step by step along the metal edge of the sunken bridge...

...a bridge that, seen from a short distance away, pointed a warning finger upward. They had named it 'Pointless.' At the apex of the incline Fern gravely stretched out a long leg and flexed her booted toe, holding her arms to the sky and revelling in her defiance of gravity while Lou caught her breath for a dizzying moment. When Fern climbed the leaning oak Lou would sit below, hugging her knees and studiously avoiding the lurch looking up would give her. Perhaps it was because of her fall from the sea wall years ago that she sometimes felt unsteady, even with both feet planted firmly on the ground.

Lou watched Fern slither down, gathering rust on her trousers. They kept a pair of boy's trousers from the jumble in their school bags and changed in the outside toilets before they left school. Fern picked her way across sand scattered with grains of coal or shale, side-stepping the remnants of planking and wooden crates along the tide line. There were broken things everywhere; broken houses, broken ships... Lou perched on the groyne and worried at a patch of barnacles with a piece of driftwood. It was warmer and her beret hung from the post next to her.

"It's a relief to say things here. Our words will be carried away by the wind and no-one will be any the wiser," she said.

Aunty Cilla and the cousins had only the clothes they stood up in when their house was bombed flat. "Just as though our time there never happened," Cousin Cissy said. It was lucky they were out collecting firewood in the old pram. No one knew whose turn would be next. "There, but for the Grace of God…" her mother repeated.

"Out here we can shout and sing and not a soul to hear us," replied Fern.

"My cousins shout every moment of the day. They don't notice other people minding about it. But I mustn't think bad thoughts about them because they've lost their father and now their home and livelihood."

"When will our real lives begin?" asked Fern.

"Perhaps these are our real lives, only we don't know it yet," said Lou.

Fern threw herself onto the sand, "Over my dead body," she groaned, rolling onto her back with a mock stab at her heart.

Lou scooped up a handful of gravelly stones and let them slip through her fingers. The cousins were the last straw. When she *was* at home the house was always full of other people's children, ones whose parents were in Mission meetings with her's. And she was expected to look after the whole brood.

This part of the shore was formed in long, dune-like ridges from the slag of an old blast furnace long gone. Carline thistles gripped the cracks, presenting a ruff of dried golden rays around a silvery centre.

"Sometimes I've had enough of doing my duty, though I know I shouldn't say so in wartime." She sighed. "Will there ever be a moment to spare for us to live our own lives? Do you think I'm a bad person to say such a thing, Fern?"

"Of course not. I whisper much worse to myself." Fern jumped up, coaxed Lou to stand and dragged her along the shingle until they were out of breath and laughing.

"But listen, Lou, you reminded me of a story our Scottish lodger told me." Fern settled herself to lie propped on her elbow along the edge of a knotty clump of sand grass. Lou checked for stones and dried sheep dottle before sitting down.

"Ready? It's called, 'The man who had no story to tell'."

They retold stories in their own way, leaving out certain details and embellishing others to suit themselves. They rehearsed to themselves during the preaching on Sundays or lying in bed before they fell asleep. Sometimes they made up long sagas or romances that continued in episodes from week to week. Fern stretched her legs along the spiky fescue and began.

"There was a man who sat at the table on the day of the feast and story telling. When the Master of the Black Arts stood on one leg and fixed

him with a gaze, he stuttered, 'I have no story to tell.' The Master pointed to the door and the man rose. All eyes were upon him as he walked outside. Snow was falling. It wasn't long before he saw ahead of him four men carrying a coffin. He joined them at the back to make a fifth. After a while they came to a churchyard. They unshouldered the coffin and slowly lowered it into the earth. As they threw on soil the man heard the priest utter his own name.

He walked on until he reached a lake with a small boat by its shore. He stepped in and began to row. Halfway across he rested the oars, looked over the side and saw a woman's face gazing at him out of the water. She rowed to the other shore of the lake where there stood a cottage in a pasture. In the cottage lived a fisherman. He took her in and gave her food and a bed for the night. They were married, lived happily for many years and were blessed with two children.

Time passed and although she loved her children, the woman felt restless. One day she climbed into the boat that was always moored near the cottage and set off back across the lake. She peered into the water and saw that the reflection staring back at her was a man's again. He retraced his steps past the place where he had seen his burial and on to the hall where the feast had been held. When he took his place at the table, the Master was still glowering at him and the people expectant. How should he begin to tell his tale?"

Lou grasped a handful of the tiny pebbles she had swept into a pile and sprayed them bouncing over the flat rocks nearby.

"Ugh. That sends shivers down your spine," she said. "I'd like to make my own future happen rather than have the 'Master of the Black Arts' make it for me."

The tide was out, almost as far as the shipping lanes. Darker streaks marked the channels that filled up first in a rush as the tide hissed back across the mud. Fern got up and stretched her legs. They made for the inshore track. They had strayed further than usual and late afternoon was turning into early evening.

"If you took a stand in life," Lou persisted, "like being a *Conchy*, you would be *making* it happen wouldn't you?"

They studied the ground as they walked. Last year Fern had almost trodden on a little black oyster catcher chick like a cotton ball peering unsteadily from a reedy patch. Their nests were hollows in the stones out in the open.

"Or perhaps it would be the saving of us to get married and away after all," Lou finished.

Fern tossed her plaits. "I'm going to marry for love which is the best possible reason," she said.

"Anyway, you feel wicked wishing for something special for yourself when everyone has to make sacrifices," Lou said. She pictured the room her mother had taken her to see, where the Czech refugees were living. They had painted it white: walls, furniture, everything. "Have you ever spoken to Marenka Vrana at school?" she asked. "One day I heard her humming a tune under her breath. I said, 'You must be happy, humming like that.' And she said, 'Oh no. It's not true. I am humming to try and make myself happy'."

Clem

The Vienna clock in the hall chimed a single stroke for 6.30a.m. Clem needed plenty of time on his first day. Still in his old donkey dressing gown he perched on the edge of the stool at the small cherry wood dressing table he used as a desk. In front of him was the diary with its black cloth binding and also the raven tin. His lesson notes and several books on the Roman Empire and the Romans in Britain were stowed in the wrinkled leather briefcase that had been his father's. His landlady, Ida Pinck, had unscrewed the dressing mirror so that he could work there in front of the window. He did not want to catch sight of his face in the glass. His owlish spectacles failed to hide the puckering he had developed above the eyebrows.

So, here he was. He had made his second break from home. Ida had been widowed before the war. In a way it was a blessing, she said, because it would have broken Pinck's heart to see a second one. He glanced at the folder containing his application for the post at St. Bede's. The name of the school had attracted him – its association with home. The folder contained his *Curriculum Vitae* and the school's letter of acceptance. He ran his eye over the CV, knowing that the *real* things were not written there: 1925 – born Clement Geoffrey Renshaw in Gosforth; 1942 – first year, degree in Architecture at King's College, Newcastle; 1943 – call-up papers and volunteered for Friend's Ambulance Unit as a conscientious objector; 1945 – post-war reconstruction work in Germany; 1947 – switched to History for final year of degree.

After that there was the gap of about a year. And he could hardly remember how he dragged himself through that final year of history. There would have been no possibility of going back to architecture. "Spineless," his father had said. Why these post-war nerves when they had survived the worst? He had managed to gloss over it at the interview; neurasthenia, soldier's heart, the doctor had said, but it wouldn't do to lose his nerve in front of a class of boys.

As he crossed the landing to the bathroom he caught strains of the song about 'H-a-r-r-eeee' from the wireless downstairs. In the bathroom he stood on the pale, black-blotched linoleum, pouching out his cheeks with his tongue in the silver speckled mirror. He wrinkled his nose at the tang of urine, sweet and occasional like salt in the wind. Near his bare toes he made out a spider hurrying along one of the cracks that scrawled across the linoleum like bits of washed up netting. A

23

low cupboard stood in one corner, white with a black line to emphasise the beading at the edge of each panel. Its door had a broken catch that swung slightly open... like the white door with the black beading on that day... the day of his tribunal. He suppressed the thought, grasped the shaving brush and busied himself soaping his jaw. The faintly antiseptic smell caught at the back of his throat. He tautened his facial muscles and drew the razor across his chin. A breath of sea in the breeze slipped through the open sash and shuffled the grey nets so they frisked at the window. Outside the perspective was flattened, washed with grey.

Back in his room he dimmed the gas light and opened the curtains to let the weak daylight filter through. Ida said Clem's rent would help her get the electric in like the people at the bottom end of the street in the new council prefabs. There would be electrical wires running over the walls like a spider web but she'd had enough of the dark ages. For the present gas light suited Clem. He preferred the yellowish glow of the flame, the feeling of hiding in the shadows. Was he really ready?

He checked: Günther's diary, Otto's raven tin and Leo's letters. Automatically, he peeped inside the diary; Etty Edelman's smaller journal lay within, slotted into the recess where the pages of the larger book had been cut in the middle. He slid the cedar box from its place on the shelf and lifted the lid. Then he replaced the books in the bottom of the box underneath the letters and lifted the tobacco tin with its

24

homemade wooden lid, ingeniously hinged; the kind of thing a soldier might carve in slack time before the big push. The design on the lid was in marquetry, a jig-saw of coloured woods depicting a raven, wings hunched and finger-feathers spread. The talonless second claw seemed incongruous. The first time he saw it he thought it looked more like a human foot. Inside were the sketches of Hitler and the bull. As a good draughtsman he appreciated the other's sharp pencil strokes. He slipped the drawing into the cedar box and the tin into his pocket.

Downstairs he poked some sticks into the range burner to keep the stove hot and boiled the kettle. His coupons helped with the rations but bacon was still scarce so he'd stick to toast for breakfast. He lit the leaky gas grill. The news on the wireless was mainly about the new Federal Republic of Germany. They played their patriotic song, *'Ich hab mich ergeben'*. He swilled the plate and cup in cold water in the washbowl, trying not to clang them against the zinc and wake Ida. The pungent smell of carbolic and the faint whiff of soda crystals dissolving jolted him sideways into a memory of washing the wounded; the man with no thigh, the one with his right arm and part of his chest gone.

Ida liked to mother him. He pulled on one of the jumpers she had knitted to bulk up under his waxed jacket. Her wardrobe was crammed with knitting wools of every ply and shade. And her penetrating eye was bright as the translucent glass swans filled with coloured waters that cast flickering sapphires and garnets onto the walls. One afternoon she showed him how the colour seeped out of snippets of dye papers and imbued the waters with emerald and ruby.

"If you've got a fear, tell me about it," she said, "and I'll knit it up into a scarf or a jumper. If you wear your fears on the outside they grow into familiar, comfortable old stuff. That way you'll get through."

It turned out he was to share a classroom. At dinner time his cohabitee, Colin Silcot, pointed out the other probationary teacher just started at the girl's school upstairs. Colin beckoned him to the half-open staff room window. The view directly opposite was of the netball court. A wavy-haired young woman in tennis skirt leapt about on the court. The children careered to and fro like bumper cars at the hoppins, their voices jangling. The young woman didn't round them up or yell instructions. She seemed unconcerned that they were taking advantage of her apparent nonchalance to wheel and spin like tops. She danced about and practised her throws into the net. Her first day and already she was acting as though what she did was the right thing to do. She had carefully chosen her position so that she would be able to see what was going on out of the corner of her eye. Could this be some kind of clever stratagem on her part?

Some of the kids were acting about, a couple imitating her. After a while they seemed bored and a bunch of them gathered around to watch. Perhaps this was how it was done; you played the part to become the real thing. He laughed inwardly; quite the opposite of his father's belief which held that acting was a sin, that there was one true self and God would find it out.

Almost as though she had just noticed the children were there she turned, called out and passed the ball to the girl who had been acting up the most.

"Three throws and pass it on," she called. The girl angled herself carefully. The others formed a line. There was some pushing and shoving. On the third throw the girl ran forward and caught the ball lightly as it came through the net and threw it to the next in line. She called out to the others as she ran to join the back of the queue but her words were lost to Clem. The girls seemed suddenly compliant.

Clem turned away, half-ashamed at watching, yet intrigued.

Later that afternoon, exhausted, he threw the briefcase onto the floor of his room. He had not been as successful as the girl on the court. He had an uneasy sense that teaching might turn out not to be his thing. He lifted *The Art of Architecture* by A.E. Richardson and Hector O. Corfiato and squinted at the diagrams and illustrations, trying to see them the way they were when life was full of plans and hope. He knew the chapters on European Architecture almost by heart as well as each of the photographic plates. Line drawings of buildings that had since been blown to smithereens were scored onto his inner eye. He had mentally ripped pages out of this book after each of the bombing raids on Hamburg, Berlin, Dresden. Even before he knew about the civilian targets he surmised enough to know that there was no real precision possible.

As a boy he was influenced by a book his father had shown him in the library of the Literary and Philosophical Society. In the rare good years when the toyshop was thriving, Ephraim took out a subscription to this library and Clem accompanied his father on visits there. This particular book was a travel journal in Latin by Wenceslas Hollar, a seventeenth century Czech artist and engraver who lived in Germany and England. Clem marvelled at the exquisite pen drawings of German landscapes, villages and towns nestling in the folds of hills, done in bistre and ink wash. Hollar had later travelled down the Rhine with the English Duke of Arundel and illustrated the journey. One day he, too, would sketch his way through the cities of Europe.

Cousin Leo said they might make a journey of discovery and find Hollar's illustrations in a museum somewhere. But first he introduced him to motorcycling, driving him in the sidecar of his *Silver Hawk*. Clem watched admiringly each time Leo kitted himself out in rubber waders, flying helmet and *Belstaff* with storm collar and straps. They planned to sketch their journey, making notes and illustrating the buildings they saw on their way.

His father's mouth curled as though he tasted sour apples when Clem mentioned their plans. As always Ephraim made his judgement plain.

"Leo has a melancholy streak," he said as though this closed down the conversation. Clem hadn't understood what his father meant until much later; it was not Leo who was melancholy, but that his presence made Ephraim despondent.

Clem treasured the photograph propped on the bookshelf. It had been taken before Leo was called up into the RAF. The pair of them, Leo tall and stooping slightly, arms over each other's shoulders like brothers, were diminished by the girth of one of the monumental criss-cross patterned pillars of Durham cathedral. His mother had exclaimed that he grew more like Leo every day and then hugged him and cried. Leo was ten years older - born in one war only to die in the next; his mother's first love, though Clem had not known it then.

Before Leo's call up, they would build model aeroplanes together in Ephraim's garden shed. In here were masculine smells of the paraffin heater and the dope used to stretch the wing-tissue taut. Now they were gathering dust in Ida's outhouse; Hurricane and Spitfire, Blenheim and Typhoon. But he could not yet let them go.

In those days architecture had fired him. The visit to St. Paul's had come at the beginning of his FAU training after studying the diagram in *Richardson* in detail, its legend learned by heart. Studying the silhouette he came to know the interplay of the horizontal and the vertical, the way the two dimensional on the page transformed into a three-dimensional figure in his mind. It took application to make himself ready for the reality; to be slotted into place over the mind's representation.

Ephraim had never spoken about the scholarship he had won, but not taken up, to study architecture at Cambridge. It had been Clem's mother, Easter, who had told him how his father's hopes had been dashed 'by life's twists and rebuffs'. But when he asked what she meant she only smiled and shook her head.

There had been one day, though, long before he had heard the name Hitler or was conscious of Germany, when his father built him a tower of teacups. His sisters and mother would have been out visiting. Father sat him at the table and Clem watched as he removed his jacket, laid it with meticulous care over the back of the settee, rolled up his sleeves and emptied the cupboard of the everyday china and the cabinet in the drawing room of the best china. Clem sat still and didn't touch as, layer by layer, the castle rose; first layers of plain green china and then the pink with the gold rims and finally the fine and delicate little floral cups that only came out for Father's important Quaker friends. Each cup was placed with the handle on his father's side.

"It's like heaven and earth," said his father, "with God at the top and then the angels and beneath them the good, each just touching the one below or above." Ephraim smiled at his son; they had a special secret.

Clem thought it best not to ask where the bad were. Instead he asked "Where are *we*, Father?" wanting to know his place in the world. He was never quite sure afterwards that he had heard the reply his father gave under his breath, "Your mother is with the bad." Ephraim stared fixedly at a turret and Clem didn't breathe a word, sensing that the words must not be acknowledged; another secret between them.

This never happened again and he didn't remember his father smiling much after that day. Occasionally, Ephraim would sit at table after a meal, preoccupied, and arrange and rearrange the cruet, milk jug and sugar bowl, all blue with a regular white stripe. His love of architecture was knotted up with God's works on earth; with man's ability to conceptualise the outward forms of perfection and recreate them in stone and brick. Clem imbibed his father's love of form, placement and proportion; though to Clem it was not worship but the reassurance of order when chaos threatened to unpick him.

There had been no money for a motorcycle tour of Europe, the opportunity for travel arriving only at the moment when Europe was splitting apart. The thrill of seeing Edinburgh and London during his Friend's Ambulance training was doused by the instability of the time. Who knew what would remain of any of these cities when the blackout curtain was unpinned and the curfew lifted?

He sifted the photographs. Here was the one of Reuben, his call up papers in the letter rack, holding up a tiny model of a spitfire in matchsticks, blackened at their tips. Reuben had slipped away in his Northumberland Fusilier's uniform after a night with Clem and Leo. They had sung together in the priory ruins, a poem by George Herbert's poem with its line; '*A man that looks on glass...*' and a Yiddish song that Reuben taught them. Reuben had been in the year above him at school and was at King's, too, reading chemistry. He was the walking companion who had guided Clem round the narrow ledge in Raven's Clough.

It had been Leo's idea to acquire a piece of candle that night, the last occasion they were all together. The flame had barely flickered, spilling a warm light from the niche as they lifted their voices in the faintly salted air. Someone hurrying along the sea front might even have heard them and paused. He had glanced back as they left and noted traces of wax in the slight depression of the sill where their candle had flamed briefly.

His father considered their night 'service' a wicked desecration and Reuben's father, Joseph, would have agreed. Ephraim said that candles in ruins were dabbling in mumbo-jumbo. He stomped upstairs leaving a moment of hush after the bedroom door shuddered into place. Later he remarked that Clem's neurasthenia was all down to his unworthiness, to his lack of faith. Leo and Reuben had stronger characters. They were the worthy ones; which made his being unscathed more bitter. His father's favouring of Leo was short-lived. Clem was better off alone now.

Home had changed when he returned from Germany. Seeing the gaps he felt his breathing sharpen as if a spelk had slipped in silently. There was a space at the bottom of Mistletoe road, another where the Spiller's factory had frowned at the quay and one where an engine yard had blocked the view from the train coming into Central Station. There were more terrible gaps in things, too: Leo, Reuben; so many wicks snuffed.

When he moved to lodgings he thought he would leave Leo's letters behind but found himself packing them into the cedar box all the same. There was a handful he read over and over. He pulled one out and read through the words he knew by heart.

Do you remember we said we would visit Europe, how we planned to visit Prague and Hamburg and Athens and Rome? I wonder what will remain of these places.

From my vantage point I sometimes catch sight of a bomber's load being jettisoned, as easy as opening a can. When you're up there you can't tell the difference between a library, a museum or someone's grand or small home. You know nothing of the small things or great things that have happened there.

I remember those drawings you used to do of St. Nicholas', The Side and the Bigg Market. Such painstaking draughtsmanship. When the buildings are gone what have we left?

He replaced the letter and his fingers slid out another. Leo's last. The final one before he had been shot down over Crete. The one with the reference to San Marino. Clem had pored over the entry in his *Everyman's Encyclopaedia*, a rocky fortress, one of the oldest states in Europe. The facility to imagine a three dimensional object had always come easily, but since the tribunal it was more than imagination. He had learned to rise above himself, becoming detached, seeing into odd crannies like the gap in the plasterwork coving where a plump spider's egg sack bulged. He moved about the globe, roaming though time. Tops of hills and mountain ranges obscured his view and drove him on further, curious to see over to the other side. Later he would remember none of the detail, but have a sense of something remaining.

It was cooler now. The afternoon sun had weakened and was tangled in the currant bushes and bird nets. The plaster crocodile on the edge of the pond lay grinning, more palely year by year as the sun blanched the green from oily jungle to water-wash temperate. He rose and slipped out of his room...

Raven

...taking in the haphazard cluttering or geometric plotting of villages, towns and cities below. From his vantage point above the mountain he saw the form crouching on its haunches as if pausing to rest. San Marino: he knew only the name, the line-drawn illustration in the *Everyman's Encyclopaedia* and where it fitted into the map of Italy. In his mind's eye a city on a rock came into being. He picked out a landing place where it seemed that the houses were leaning their heads together conferring. This was a city occupied by refugees, where someone might lose himself in the shadows as a cart heaped with straw rattled by, a place that could withstand siege. Long before people settled there, water had dissolved the interior and gutted the mountain like a whale. Afterwards, they mined its limestone to the bone, so caverns and quarries lay beneath churches and civic buildings, proof against battering from above; air raid shelters crafted out of a mountain.

It was a place that invited strong opinions. Some shook their heads and frowned at a church spire high enough to scratch the belly of the sky; others despised it as a hotbed of corruption. Everything could be found there, from carter's boots to ladies' pigskin slippers and fat merchants purses.

On the day of The Tribunal the inhabitants entered a cave, filing in by rank. Before him was a small arena, the Sculpture Well. Clem was relieved it was not a sacred place. Instead the well contained a stone carving of six lexicographers and six architects, each holding their books and pens, set squares and compasses; each beleaguered by a horned, hoofed or scaly beast adorned with a riot of trees and flowers which grew from their backs. As he watched, the beasts opened their spine-toothed mouths, belched flame and began consuming the pages of the scholar's books.

The people met in the cave to tell their stories to each other and to Raven who presided over the meeting, the hood of her black feathered cloak drawn back to reveal her wrinkled face. Clem knew his turn would come. A candle near him guttered and wax congealed on the sill. What was it they wanted him to tell: of reading *Hakluyt's Voyages* under the covers; of tuning secretly to Louis Armstrong on his crystal set to avoid his father's wrath, wrath that would always congeal in the same look of disappointment? Each look pointed to the glut of Clem's failures souring on the pantry shelf. Should he tell them the story of Ephraim's disgust when he caught his son baking pies with his mother, an apron tied around his waist?

"That's the only architecture you'll ever do, the styling of a fluted pie crust."

Clem had looked at his arms, shirt sleeves rolled up, freckles blotted, a smear of raw sugar and butter across his cheek and chin. His father turned his back. Perhaps he should recount his tribunal plea. It had satisfied the panel, but not his father; he had given the wrong grounds; moral rather than religious.

The candles flickered and Raven unpinned her black feather hairpiece, letting the hair underneath tumble in soft white falls like his Grandmother's. Her dark bird skin crumpled in folds. Her eyes were dusk grey and, as he plumbed their depths, it was as if he were looking back at himself.

"I have no tale to tell" he heard himself say.

Raven, veiled in luxuriant white hair to the hooked claws, stood on one Jack-booted foot and pointed a berry-skin fingernail towards the dark outside. He rose and lurched with a pang of nausea, holding out his hand to steady himself but his fingers found no comforting chair, jacket slung over the back, only a rough limestone surface. He turned to look back as a great door slammed against him; a white panelled door with black beading... Georgian probably...

Outside, the sky was choked with flurrying flakes that blurred the rocky descent. A little ahead he could make out the movement of trudging figures, heads bowed as they shouldered what appeared to be a coffin. One of the bearers turned to face him and he recognised Leo and someone else whose gait was familiar. Thank God.

"Leo." he called, "Reuben, wait!" But his feet sank further into the deepening snow with every step. Leo turned away without a sign of recognition. Reuben did not turn round. Clem struggled to follow, gaining gradually on the procession. He moved to take his place at the back of the coffin, falling naturally into the pace of the others. The box was heavy, even though there were four other bearers. They climbed the steep track. Leo walked next to him but they exchanged no words. The telegram must have been a terrible mistake. Here he was and the others, too; Clem sensed he knew them all. The bear-like form at the front whose height unbalanced the coffin, tipping it back towards Clem, was Günther, he felt sure. The slight figure must be his brother, Otto. When they reached the dry-stone wall of the small churchyard they eased their burden to the ground. The mourners' faces were covered as, from under their cloaks, they unstrapped spades.

"At least this soldier got back to the mountain to die," said a young woman pushing back her cowl.

"He's not quite a soldier, though," said another. "He was wearing khaki when we laid him out but there were red crosses on his shoulder tabs."

Leo turned to Clem and smiled ruefully, "What a waste - all that promise. He was going to be an architect, to change the world, you know."

Clem felt uneasiness in the pit of his stomach. Who had the soldier been?

As a child, Clem had felt loss when a column of sunlight vanished. The feeling stirred in him now. Here lay a man who would never again touch homely objects, a cream jug held lingeringly by rough hands, cut and red from scouring and scrubbing.

Another woman pushed back her hood and rolled up the loose sleeves of her cloak. Her hair was glossy black, almost as purple as raven feathers and her forearms strong and muscular. She scored the close-nibbled fescue of the high pasture with her spade, slicing into the topsoil to gain some purchase in the stony layer below. Clem took his spade and hacked at the earth. After half an hour's hard labour they had dug the grave. Now perhaps he would hear the name of the soldier spoken by the priest.

He recognised one of the girls he had glimpsed pacing the length of the sands as he flew low over the coast and out to sea.

The priest's face was folded and weathered; his father's eyes. "Ashes to ashes, dust to dust." He intoned the words of the Burial of the Dead and then the name of the dead soldier. The name shot volts of electricity into Clem. There was a snort of suppressed laughter and he looked up into the young, delicately freckled face of his mother, framed by the hood which she now pushed back. He reached out to her but she scampered away, looking back as though taunting him like a child playing tag.

Earth and scree clunked onto the wooden coffin and the mourners, some, faces still covered, huddled close to each other. Those who had brought spades scraped a mixture of soil and stones back into the grave. Clem looked around for Leo and Reuben, but they were nowhere to be seen. In the red scar of a high clough above he made out that someone was inching around a precipitous ledge.

The mourners dispersed to perch on rocks or squat on the ground. A woman with one front tooth missing and a long face like a horse tossed her dark mane and snorted, tucked up her tunic in her undergarments and begun to dance and sing a song popular with the underground movement, "Can you strut the strut that Mussolini struts?"

"Take it away, Lili," chorused others.

Lili lifted her nose in the air, sniffed and crumpled her face with mock disgust. She, too, reminded him of his mother when they used to sing and laugh together in the late afternoon, his father away at the toyshop.

"Another one done, then," said a woman with tar stained fingers and teeth, rolling a cigarette. She wiped the sweat from her forehead. Her face, too, struck a chime, "He's quiet now." She rolled up her cloak to her knees and rubbed her shins.

"War – it makes fools of the lot of us."

There were murmurs of assent. Clem watched a lizard scuttle into the shade of a rock.

"I'd say one old Dictator's about as bad as another," she continued. "It's the adulation they want. Fingering the crowd brings their limp winkles to attention. They want to be the matinee idol of every woman and revered by every man. Two tough old fowls is one too many cocks of our farmyard."

"Tell us the story of the turkey and that old peacock we kept a few years back, Eva," said the woman with raven-feather hair. Eva stubbed out her roll-up and pressed the unsmoked butt into a tin decorated with a marquetry inlaid raven. There were curious scratches inside the lid.

Eva picked up Clem's expectant look. "We're living in the fag end of the world. Aesop got in before us and stole all the best stories."

"It happened in our yard... we're living in Aesop's world, only most of us don't see it," said raven-feather hair.

"Yeah, go on, Eva; give us, 'The Turkey and the Peacock'."

"I might, if you're good girls."

"That counts us out, then," they laughed.

"I saw this happen when butter wouldn't melt in my mouth and I've been to Rome and back to tell it to the Pope three times since," Eva began.

"Aye and stolen the tiles from the floor to prove it."

The others laughed raucously.

"The hens and ducks were head over heels in hot pursuit of their adored Adolfus, that old peacock we had. Hypnotised by his piercing cry and the crimson and electric blue eyes in his feathers, they hung on every word of his rousing speeches. That is, all except for Benito, the turkey, who was crazed with jealousy. He wanted no less than all eyes idolising him; he'd

41

make the fools admit he was superior. He swore to be Adolfus'
downfall in talon to talon combat. But he wasn't tough enough
to go it alone against the other cocks, so time went by and
Benito resigned himself to making a pact with Adolfus."

The afternoon sun cast shadows of stones across the
graveyard. The priest, leaning against a gravestone, had nodded
off, his arms folded across his chest.

"Old Adolfus was always ripping strips off all comers,
aiming to get his claw into someone else's farmyard,"
continued Eva, "so he set up the 'Pact of Spurs' so he and his
turkey friend could nail the other cocks."

Lili gave the thumbs sign and they all laughed.

"The peacock was the elder bird and all this armed combat
caused his ticker to peter out, so he lay down on his favourite
perch one day and gave up the ghost. The hen told the geese
that their old Generalissimo would blow his horn no more."

The women's laughter was infectious. Clem glanced up. The
figure in the gorge was almost out of sight.'

"Meanwhile no-one told Benito of his rival's demise. He
happened by on one of his reconnaissance patrols and saw his
so called ally apparently asleep, so he seized his chance and
attacked in a flurry of feathers. The peacock stared through
glazed eyes for all the world as if he were asleep. Benito, the
brave, placed his claw triumphantly on Adolfus' neck, a gesture
worthy of an Emperor."

"Go for it Benito." someone shouted.

The sun had come up and was burning the back of Clem's neck. There was no sign of a climber in the gorge. Perhaps he had better be on his way…

…to where, descending towards his room, he caught the glint of a ruby eye of the plaster owl on the landing table outside his room.

October

Lou

Lou pedalled the length of the prom. The pier, its ballroom balanced on the far end like a battered biscuit tin, had grown shabbier lately. Further out was quicksand where people could slip away without trace. Long ago, she and Fern used to criss-cross the tide line, their footprints undone by each tide. Along the bay they were clearing the signs of war; the wrecked concrete hulks, people said, were coal barges. She would never again hear the strains of her father's concertina as the Mission Band played from *Songs of Glory* on the sands. The turquoise tweed skirt he had bought her was rolled and tucked into her satchel along with notebooks, books and pencils. The old trench coat, unbuttoned, flapped in the wind and, as she neared the school gates, she was conscious that Aunt Beryl's marbled silk stole had come loose and was trailing behind her.

Beryl had also given her the Elswick Hopper bicycle. It was more elegant than the common or garden models, painted cream and green rather than the usual black. It jolted her over the cinder walk towards the bike sheds at the back of the school. The red bricks were a façade; the sides and back a coarse yellow-grey brick. This was the old boy's school building, now shared with the girls whose building had been bombed; boys downstairs and girls upstairs. She negotiated the corner, her bike wobbling at the right-angled bend before the cycle shed; a long, low concrete affair, crouching like 'Last Watch Barge'...

...where she sat, her sketchpad propped on her knees. People said the barnacled platform was an inner shell of concrete from a coal barge. Three of them would surface each low tide. This one was stable so they could scramble on from the rocks where it had grounded on one side. They sat along the edge overlooking a rectangular well with an iron bar running across the centre. Lou stuck the tip of her tongue between her teeth. The horizon was more difficult to draw than you would imagine, perhaps because it was not a boundary, but a fuzzy join where two elements merged. She moved the lines slightly using her old India rubber but the graphite traces from earlier shading blurred the boundary more and more.

Fern looked up from squinting at her own drawing; a mass of dried white cells - cuttlefish or octopus eggs. She crawled over on all fours and squinted at Lou's sheet, "You're scribbling forwards and backwards... like the front line," she said.

"Oh that's just lines on maps. This is a different sort of line."

Fern stood up, stretched and spread her arms wide. She rose balletically on the toes of her sandshoes, pointed one foot and placed it on the iron bar. She steadied herself and took the few steps across the bar, placing one foot in front of the other expertly.

"Supposing you lived under the line?" she asked, looking back from the other side of the concrete rim of the well.
Lou sighed. "Fern, you're blotting out my horizon."

"The space belongs to all of us," cried Fern in a theatrical voice, throwing up her arm against the sky. "I wonder if Hitler had been a woman whether things would have been different - Adeline Hitler!" She put her nose in the air and pranced along the far edge of the barge with a waggle.

Lou laughed. She shaded the water surface pierced by a marooned branch, its reflection zig-zagging back on itself.

"I saw an old man standing on a crate by the pier yesterday," she said. "My father was playing with the army band after meeting. The old fellow was a pacifist. He talked about Mahatma Gandhi putting a clay compress on a goat's ankle in the middle of a war council."

She outlined a long streak of cloud with the stub of soft pencil that had lasted her for two years. Fern lowered herself over the side of the well and lay peering into the gloom. As her eyes focused she could see that it was awash with crabs and sea urchins, fish feeding too far in, trapped till next tide.

"You've got an aunt out in India haven't you Lou?"

"Aunty Beryl. I used to think I wanted to be Beryl; all those silks and servants. My mother says it will be hard for her to settle back here if they have to leave India."

When Aunty Beryl came to England a year ago she rented a cottage in Cornwall and Lou spent a few weeks there. She had been there when the men delivered a big Indian trunk with iron straps; full of things her aunt wanted to save if the Japanese invaded India. Lou pulled out a shimmering piece of silk, the colour of the iron filings they had set light to in science at school. Her aunt showed her how to wrap it round to make a sari, though there was far too much material and it trailed behind her. She had paraded around the cottage garden in it, ceremoniously clasping the dark gold elephant god pot.

"Beryl says India is like a pot on the boil."

Fern sat up and pulled her knees towards her, wrapping her arms around them. "You remember Mr Meek taught our class that Gandhi visited the Lancashire cotton mills with his distaff and round spectacles just after we were born. He came to tell the poor here about the poor in India; how they want to make and sell their own cotton. And he told the mill children he loved them as if they were his own?"

"Gandhi's the opposite to Hitler, isn't he? Being patriotic by peaceful means, not force; loving his country without hating another. But father says he's a realist." Lou shivered. The sky had clouded over. They packed the pencils and sketchpad in Fern's satchel. "Even so, if we were German we wouldn't be allowed to tell the truth and love our enemy," she finished. There would be a bowl of soup for the helpers at the soup kitchen tonight and she would swallow a cup of tea with a hunk of bread from the scullery beforehand. They slithered down the side of the barge.

"How long do you suppose your Aunty Beryl and Uncle Fergus will hold out in India?" asked Fern.

"Not long. I don't know. Beryl said if India did get independence or became a dominion Uncle Fergus would lose his job. He'd probably get a post in the Civil Service over here. Their twins have run wild and led the servants a dance, my mother says, so they would have to be subdued and learn English refinement."

Fern put her nose in the air and minced across the rocks on tiptoe. "Refined. Like us," she said, turning to Lou.

Lou held an invisible cup to her lips, "I'd rather sit in the sun in a warm climate and sip Indian tea with Gandhi from dainty china teacups instead of utility. Heavenly."

...As she rounded the corner into the bike shed she realized someone else was already here – one of the men from the boy's school in motorcycle dress, bright red hair rumpled.

Clem

The *Silver Hawk* had rumbled through lanes hung with applewood smoke and dusty blackberries, the ground strewn with horse chestnuts brought down in last night's wind. As he rode Clem imagined Leo as a bird of prey; silent, accurate and alone. When Leo hitched the sidecar to his motorcycle they flew together, connected by a thread. But that had been before the war

During Leo's last leave, Clem overheard him speaking to his mother. Ephraim must have been out as, by then, Leo was no longer welcome in his father's presence. He had gone downstairs and caught sight of them through the crack where the Best Room door stood ajar. Easter stroked Leo's head as he leaned against her, almost unthinkable in Ephraim's house.

Clem retreated a safe distance back up the stairs and eavesdropped.

He heard Leo say, "It's all right." Then he told Easter that he preferred being alone, self-reliant, everything depending on his own split-second thinking up there in the skies away from all the mess down below. Surprisingly, there was a sound of sobbing, then his mother quietly comforting his cousin. Later, when the crying subsided, Clem came downstairs and sat with them for a time. He noticed the papery greyness of Leo's skin. The first time in a *Hurricane*, he told them, he took off in panic with the dark forms of *Messerschmitts* in the corner of his eye. With the *Spitfire* panel in front of him he knew by touch where all the switches were, even in pitch darkness.

"I smell it in my dreams," he said, "hot, thick vapours of kerosene, oil and cordite. Those smells clog your mouth and you wake up wanting to wretch with the pungency of it." Leo laughed a queer laugh, putting on a good show about how his helmet was tipping across his eyes and there wasn't time to adjust it as he yanked the canopy across. The *Hurricane* made a wasp whine, a different more anxious sound than the *Spitfire*. He had clipped the lid in place, but still felt vulnerable as if in a glasshouse, the cockpit more exposed than the *Spitfire's*. He fumbled for switches. Clem imagined the blood pulsing in his ears and Leo repeating out loud, "Get me out of this one and I'll never stray, be a good son and love my enemy."

*

Here I go again, Clem thought. It was as though he could relive the moments suggested by Leo's letters more vividly than he allowed himself to revive his own moments of terror. He was not sure he would keep the model planes much longer; like his books on architecture they belonged to a different person. Sometimes, though, he needed to be with Leo, to be able to see from Leo's bird's eye view.

He wheeled the *Silver Hawk* into the bike shed, a concrete roof and back with a row of metal slots to stand bicycles or motorcycles. Most of the teachers cycled, though the Deputy Head and Head of Science in the boys' school had cars; a *Ford Popular* and a *Morris Minor*. Someone at the girls' school had an old *Singer*. Clem untied his fleece-lined cap and stood feeling the breeze in his hair. He glanced at the briefcase perched upright and neatly roped on the rack at the back of the bike; still there.

He stood a moment searching his pockets for the tin of *Old Holborn* and matches. He liked to give himself enough time to roll a cigarette before he braved the boys' school staff common room. Colin Silcot had it in for him. He had overheard him on yard duty holding forth about how he'd been called up as a Bevan Boy, done his bit. There'd been no choice for him, not like those pacifist namby-pambies. Did he sense that Clem had been a Conscientious Objector? Or did he know despite Clem's buttoned lip. He should come clean and clear the air.

51

The match flared. He cupped his hands and sheltered it from the breeze. Cigarette in mouth, he wiped his specs on the rag stuffed in his pocket for the purpose. A pair of goggles might stop them steaming up in this moist weather. He noted the damp patches on his flying jacket and leggings; they were due for another waxing.

A cyclist rounded the corner, her silky scarf fluttering behind. Her bike wobbled to a halt at the other end of the shed. She jumped with practised ease, one foot on either side before extracting a leg. Clem noticed the leather satchel and tennis racquet she unstrapped from the back. It was the young woman he had watched practising netball with her class a couple of weeks ago.

"Could do better," she said. "I've been practising that manoeuvre."

"Yes. Dismounting is the tricky bit," he said. He looked more closely at the bicycle. "An Elswick Hopper, isn't it?"

"Yes. It belonged to my aunt. She came back from India after the war and decided she would become a little less memsahib and more down to earth. I ferreted it out from the things in her shed. Is it a good one?"

He crouched down and looked it over appreciatively.

"They're hand built. Nice long shape."

He stood up, cinched his slim rollup butt between his fingers and slipped it into his top pocket. He took out another cloth and gave the *Hawk* a wipe over before unroping the briefcase.

She smiled.

"Well, must fly. I'm Louisa Rainbird, just started at the girls' school."

"Clement Renshaw." He extended his hand. "History. Boys' school."

At home that afternoon he stood in the bathroom overlooking the garden. He could see where Ida and her cousin Violet had the card table set up and a pot of tea stewing on the stone ledge that ran around the edge of the pond. The shadows were sharp as though sliced with a paper knife. Words from Leo's letter grumbled unasked for in his thoughts...

...if you were here in happier times we would drop small stones off bridges or sit in the shade of a gypsum column at Knossos where the sun slices the roof shadows like a paper knife – no shadow of a Messerschmitt.

You'd feel a presence here as if the land itself is breathing. We'd visit the hill people I've met. And you too might, round some corner, come upon Odysseus tricking Polyphemos...

He grappled the chain and water swilled the toilet bowl. He had visited the *Laing Art Gallery* with his father once... that time after the school toilets... The cistern trickled as it filled and the memories opened up. Everyone knew his father was a

53

Conchy. He remembered the rusting pipes, the ancient cistern and the clanging chain. They held him down there so long he had thought he was drowning. The worst of it wasn't so much the smell or even the foul faeces cloying in the back of his throat...

"Shove him down again. It's his just deserts. His father wanted our fathers to die for his freedom."

"Tell us what your father is." Clem was sure he knew that voice. He kept his peace. "Shove him down again. Your father is a coward. Repeat after me, 'My father is a coward'."

"Say it. Say it! My father got his legs blown off for the likes of you."

He was in no position to argue. The bell for class clanged. The Latin master's voice roared. He was yanked upright.

"Ah, Renshaw, is it? And the usual culprits. Stay where you are, you lot. Get your hands off your face, boy. I'll whack your persecutors," he said, "for misuse of school property. But as for you, Renshaw, I'll whip you to within an inch of your life. I know what you are. Now wash your head. You smell foul. And get to your class."

That evening when Clem arrived home with the smell still on him, his father had been as angry and distant as growling thunder. He said nothing, gave no advice, offered neither comfort nor embrace. But a few days later he had taken him to the *Laing*. He marched steadily towards the John Martin exhibition; past the Northumbrian landscapes to the vision of the flood and the destruction of Sodom.

"There," said Ephraim, triumphantly, as they stood before the terrifying proportions of the hall where Belshazzar's feast was depicted. "He may have been a country lad born down the road in Haydon Bridge but Newcastle was only a train ride away, even then. He saw what cities are - and what they might be." Ephraim said no more than this. Like his mother, Clem knew there could be no conversation. The thought of his mother brought up another feeling of guilt. They shared the same inadequacy in Ephraim's eyes.

There was a pause in the scrabble game in the garden below as Ida puzzled over her letters. Occasionally Clem caught a phrase or two through the open window.

"...all right up there, poor soul?" Ida's intonation left the question lingering in the air.

They'd insisted he have the doctor for the nightmares and the shouting out in the night. Doctor Sevitski had said Clem wasn't the only one. Even after five years some still cried out for a lost friend in the night.

Voices inhabited his consciousness. "...*Conchies* did their bit... *Conchies*..."

"...your move, dear..."

"...queer collection... up my sleeve... ancient Greeks..."

"...chimera?"

"Chimera – monster... serpents tail..."

"Are you stuck, dear?"

"…my old dad, Ida… couldn't abide *Conchies*… First War… hands on deck."

"…old Tom, eh…"

"…proud man …wasn't a bully at the start …siege of Mafeking."

"Mafeking…"

"…only girls …knew nothing then."

"…had a drubbing, well and good… starvation diet… months, see… pals at Colenso… knocked the stuffing out… I say the stuffing…"

Clem parted the nets and peered beyond the two women. The garden had lines that gave it a sense of balance, even stillness. He began calculating angles; the wooden frame of the unoccupied deckchair. There were curves too, suggesting movement, like the scoop of the green and yellow striped canvas suspended by the gooseberry bushes.

The women's voices sailed through the September evening like birds dipping and skimming, now closer, now just a faraway spec tossed on the wind…

Raven

....above him as he reached a summit and saw that the actual summit was further away than ever. He climbed by a rocky path, hewn in some places into rough steps and in others cracked by winters of ice into a layered, step-like formation. Climbing was hot work. There were times when he was not sure whether he was running away or hurrying to meet someone, only that he could not stop. The air was still, holding its breath, only occasionally punctured by the vibrating hum of insects. He had the sensation of being drawn on.

Clem remembered tramping through valleys, the hairs on his back sensing long ago border wars; even the rocks seeming charged. Now he scrambled onto a small plateau, plunging upwards into the air as he reached the flat surface.

*

Away to the south parachutes flocked like thistledown, their silk taut in the wind. He moved closer, among them, recognising their uniforms. They drifted downward in the shimmering heat; terror, mingled with a palpable sense of glory, pulsing through the air. Clem breathed and felt a vein in Günther's neck swell. In the moments before he slammed into the present, time slowed, stretched and the sun sweated oils from his neck and onto the collar of his uniform. He was dazzled by the intensity of blues and greens below as sea and land lurched towards him.

Suspended from strings and dotted amongst his falling compatriots were rough, cracked wooden figures, slapped with patches of grey and flesh-coloured paint. The *Oberstleutnant* had told them there would be hundreds of men, bobbing and drifting down wind, augmented by decoy dolls. After the heat and fumes of the plane, the jump into the arms of the enemy, adrenaline coursed through him. There were splashes as paratroopers hit the water while planes grumbled above.

Higher still, Raven was making her way south. Below, Clem spied a small boat. He telescoped in towards a moving mass in the stern which resolved into grizzled brown sheep chewing at something sprouting from the boat's timbers. They nosed a heap of red-bronze fish piled in the front. Clem lowered himself onto the wooden seat, nudging a beast out of the way. It was a small caique, well tarred and caulked in the manner of the islands. Around him the sea breathed softly. He took up the oars, dipped them, and began to pull, leaning his back into the work, feeling a tensing and slackening of sinews and the stretch of his muscles.

The horizon expanded at the far edges of a surface, taut as a drum. On the other side of the island ocean swell billowed but here in the Sea of Crete it was calm. Momentarily, Clem watched a body rotate in the centre of a frilling parachute like a dead jellyfish; translucent concentration of sea spread out on the surface. Then the pale face slipped under.

He secured the oars in the rowlocks, allowing the boat to drift and meditated, watching light curl from the surface. Leaning over, he caught his reflection; something about it distinctly more... not feminine, yet female. She checked no-one was behind, looking over her shoulder, and touched her face. Her skin was soft, without bristles, with a different definition; no six-o-clock shadow of stubble. Was it just this and the fuller sweep of her hair? Her arms were still pale and freckled. She ran her hands over her waist and hips, feeling the heavier roundedness of her lower body. Had she fallen asleep? Could this face in the water be hers? If she slipped through this country in disguise perhaps she would find an answer to the question that whined like a fly trapped in her ear.

Far above, green, red and yellow silks ballooned open. Around her canvas flopped onto the surface and saturated. A cough and a curse broke the silence. Men freed themselves from the tangle of ropes and dived under, a school of seal bodies.

*

Günther thought of his sister, Eva, and of another face... a woman's face, eyes deep in the shadow of their hollows. He pressed fists into his salt-brimmed eyes, imprinting the white island onto the back of his lids.

The *Junker Fifty-Two*'s engines groaned. Otto fell in October sunlight, the wake-up pills kicking his body into alertness. Sensations and thoughts tumbled rapidly one after another. Filthy black smoke intermittently rolled back to uncover chaos below. Incendiaries and advance dive bombers had fired up a raging blaze. His heart palpitated, a pinball juddering between obstacles. If this was to be his end it was true history; not trapped between the pages of a mouldy parchment. He was the inheritor and protector of civilization, saving it from this degenerate people; goats and Cretans crawled like maggots on the hillside above.

The smell and choking smoke from below threatened to engulf him, but he seized the image of the castle at Heidelberg, tier on tier of stone columns and recessed statues of knights and kings, and then recalled his black-clad grandmother. He blazed with love for his country, for the *herrenvolk*. Those documents had been lies; he could feel the purity of his Aryan blood pulsing in him as sharp as the scorching flare that caught his arm before he fell free of the blaze.

*

60

Soldiers from New Zealand and Britain manned the trenches together. Fishermen, herdsmen and farmers, butchers, bakers and builders, their backs to the mud, cocked guns and shot at the flock blotting out their sky. Yesterday, Rhavamanthys, the stone-carver, lashed oxen to a great rock and directed them to heave it to her workshop. Today, her eyes bulbous and veined with smoke, she took aim, delivered a round and reloaded. German boys dropped like wildfowl, their migration arrested. Stavros heaved bodies into piles, registering the cracks and blasts of Bren guns, rifles and Bofors amongst the deafening rattle.

She let slip a page and was alone again, floating towards a cove. The sheep buffeted the side of the boat restlessly. Looking from the edge of the water her eye traced the curve of the breakers splashing a pebbled beach. Beyond, a steep line of rocky cliffs sloped upward towards a wood of olive and cypress. She felt comfortable in her female guise; curious about her body, but not awkward. She picked up the oars and began to test out her new frame. Her arms were less powerful but she had strength across her shoulders and back.

The turquoise sky darkened with a slash of purpley-pink to the west. A cool wind flapped her dress against her body. Time had passed; she didn't want to be caught out on the sea with only a glimmer of moon to guide her. She began rowing more quickly now, leaning into the movement of the boat. As the boat drew closer to the pebbly shore she fixed her eye on cypresses fingering the gathering dusk. She landed the boat to one side of a ridge of rocks extending into the sea. Not far away a flat platform of rocks was split to form a narrow funnel. Muffled cries from that direction resonated on the surface.

How buoyant the body was here, thought Günther, and yet you might tire of kicking against the swell and let it salt your lungs.

The matted-woolly sheep lumbered onto the shore and made towards a track that wound its way up the side of the cliff. As Clem traced their path, her hand shading her eyes, she noticed what looked like a pile of clothes lying not far off; a neatly folded pile of slate grey trousers and jackets, German army issue. Beside one of them was a bundle. It stirred as she approached. Peering more closely at it in the dusk, she saw the lean face of a tiny baby yawn and beat its arms.

A movement caught her eye on the flat rocks between her and the swimmers. A group of women crouched there, one with her arms around the shoulders of a woman on either side. Their forearms and wrists were very thin, their grey tunics loose around them. One woman held her hand over the mouth of the one in the centre. Another in front bent down. The one in the middle seemed in pain. She doubled over. After a moment she lifted a tiny wrinkled body, the chord still attached. She stooped again and Clem wondered if she had bitten through the chord. Then she turned the child over and slapped it. Clem felt a vague sense of shame at witnessing something so private. The child that lay in the bundle began to cry. Close to its arms lay a pile of guns.

Clem turned away and paused to find her bearings. A susurration of sea through pebbles and an intermittent bleat gave away places where sheep had settled on the margin of the beach. Ahead of her a handful of sheep lumbered to their feet and skittled in several directions as she approached. As her eyes adjusted to the faint moonlight she followed a couple of animals along a track. Occasionally she stumbled and her hands met earth and grasped twisted olive roots.

The path opened after a time into steeply inclined pasture surrounded by cypresses and thorny bushes. Clem held her breath, sensing a watcher. There was a light at the other side of the clearing. She let herself be guided by it, past the hulks of sheep breathing nearby, towards the figure who loomed from behind a candlelit lamp. The slight stoop, as if bending to the height of the rest of mankind, reminded her of someone.

"L-Leo - you're here," she found herself stuttering. But when he lifted the lamp she saw it was not him. Unfamiliar hollows of shadow caressed this face as the light swayed. The man turned, swinging the lamp with him, illuminating the white of a cottage wall. Inside, he threw his headscarf onto a hook by the door.

"I am Günther," he said, his voice a low growl.

He was tall and dark and as on edge as a bear sniffing threat; waiting. He laid his arm protectively around Clem's shoulder and pulled her into the light, the skin on his arms silver-pale against his dark hair.

The room was a jumble of urns, pots, stacks of newspapers, books and an easel with several sheets of drawings attached. Sketched on these were detailed copies of stone decorations, carvings from the capitals of pillars, bosses, pier decorations, mosaics, fragments of Egyptian and Islamic style ornament, Minoan and Mycenaean pots, Greek and Romanesque finials and friezes. In the corner a desk held an upright black *Underwood* typewriter, like the one in the corner of Leo's room. Günther hung a sooty kettle over glowing embers, part-banked with leaf mould. As he pulled off his black leather boot a cake of red clay rolled onto the hearth. Clem sensed another presence in the room. She turned and noticed a child observing her in silence, face lowered.

"This is Mirrie," said Günther. "When I found her she fitted into a drawer lined with an old vest. She looked like a Turkish raisin, small enough to hold in the palm of my hand.

"Her mother's milk curdled in her body."

Clem thought of the child near the swimmers on the rocks.

"Do you know what *'sprachregelung'* is?" Günther asked. "…well-spoken killers, a form of words sugaring their tongues, good tailoring, clean boots and a good address…"

As he spoke, he slid sheets of paper from the easel, arranged them on the floor and began to work. He pushed a hinged ruler toward Clem. Clem unfolded and rotated the parts as though familiar with the object.

"A new city should have no good addresses," said Günther. Mirrie squirmed off her chair and moved across the floor like a breath of air, pausing to let her fingers stray over objects, a white feather, a piece of broken terracotta.

The sheets smelt of his hair, of tea leaves and moss, his form in the bed a long ridge of hills. In the morning he brought strong black coffee and bread, his hair damp, a trickle of black dye trailing down his cheek. She felt light headed. The chest in the bedroom was packed with embroidered skirts, shawls and black headscarves. Günther opened the cupboard to reveal dark suits and an ancient military uniform decorated with red braiding.

"Take what you like," he said, "you'll need to blend in."

In another cupboard were four inch mortars in long cylindrical cases, two-pounder field guns and tins of petrol.

"Salvage," he said. "When we Germans dropped them to supply the Nazi troops they were scattered over the island. The British were fleeing at the time."

Clem peered inside pots and jars half-filled with shards of pottery and ran her finger along the sharp edge of torn fragments of metal, sea-scoured wood, shell cases and shrapnel.

Günther opened the back door and went out. She heard the pocking sound of an axe before it bites, then a splitting of fibres. She stepped outside onto uneven flags and inspected the wooden figures leaning casually against a wall, grooved along the grain and charred. Half-made fishing nets were draped over them. Clem had a moment of unsteadiness, a sensation of falling through salted air before Günther straightened up from his work.

"Driftwood," he said.

Over the next few days Clem took a turn at the watch. The sea was lighter near the shore. Inland, the movement of birds against ochre and reds was hard to pick out. She trained her eye. Sometimes she saw, or thought she saw, a movement high up. She was watchful inside the house too. On the windowsill was a vase of dusty white gull feathers, the kind girls gave to lovers reluctant to sign up in the Great War, the sort posted through the letterboxes of conchies. One day she came across a book of ciphers and a scrumpled copy of an *Anti-Conscription Pledge* hidden away beneath cookery magazines.

The following day there was knock at the door. Clem watched through the frame of an open shutter as Mrs

Oikonomou heaved the dead weight of the sheep off her back. Sweat oiled the gully between her breasts. She spat on Günther's hot doorstep,

"Another one strayed onto my land. Shot by one of those butchers," she said. "They don't always shoot straight so I finished their shoddy work." She glanced around at the muddle of the room. "My daughter has some news from the Dovecote," she said. "Cowards, those boys who pay for her body."

She looked meaningfully at Clem "And he's a dark one. German pacifist?" She turned back to Günther. "Those Nazi shits beat Rhavamanthys to within an inch of his life when he refused to carve a party eagle for the headquarters."

In time Clem's watch took her further afield. She was not the only one who registered the tremor of the landscape. She stood in a field of long white radishes, easing them from the earth, crumbling it away with her fingers, her baby strapped into a basket on her back. Her mother turned and looked back. Her face was lined. German soldiers were guarding the road, restricting movement around the island. One of them pointed at the hillside with his gun, saying, "This place is unstable."

Clem knew that the soldier's unease was not only with the landscape. He could not understand her country. It was an alien place to him: the slow baking heat that charred their skins, the paint for their boats mixed with earth ochres, the walls that grew out of rock. For their own part they allowed the Germans to think of them as cattle; uncomprehending, if insolent. Let them think of their homes as stables to shit in.

Clem knelt and tugged at a radish, coaxing it out, stalks pinched between finger and thumb where they joined the root. Her scraped knees were padded by a coarse, black skirt. Both women filled their flat baskets. She knew by her stiffened neck that her mother felt the eyes of the German bastards on her. She squinted at the younger boy. A ewes-milk face but curdled, facial hair a downy froth. What did her father say, "Without my beard I would be undressed." The thought of Spiros during the last days at Suda bay made her pause. She had barely recognised him afterwards, except for his beard.

"Get her out of here," the medics shouted. But her mother had refused to leave the cave without him, without his body.

"He was dead when we got him here," the nurse told her.

Clem picked her way over to a wall, sat down heavily and opened her dress. Her mother kept her eye on the soldiers and spat at the dust. The child's father had disappeared. The Nazis said those wiped out had never existed. As the child suckled, Clem kept one eye on the German with the gun.

Moving closer, Otto peered at the baby's face. Its eyes were screwed up; small mouth, thin lips, lolling tongue.

"Bad blood," he muttered, glaring at her child, "bad blood." Otto levelled the gun and screwed up his eye. He indicated with the butt of the gun that she should lay the child on the ground, but Clem hugged the child to her, feeling its warm, milky breath.

He stepped forward. With one hand he held his gun to the woman's head and with the other grasped a piece of her dress and wrenched it downward. He felt a jolt as his gun barrel was knocked to one side and smashed up against his face. The breath momentarily knocked out of him, he fell. His brother stood over him.

"You have no authority." Günther said

Otto raised his upper body onto his elbows.

"Authority? All we get are confused orders. The place is out of order; orders come from here, there everywhere. Chaos!" Tears prickled the corners of his eyes. "We are fighters for a German people's revolution. This is the imperial project. An empire for the ordinary Germans... I don't want to fuck her if that's what you think."

Günther shifted his gun and Otto sat up, brushing soil from his sleeves.

Clem turned to go. 'Bad blood'. She had heard those words in English, not long ago. Another word surfaced from a pamphlet on Ephraim's desk; 'Eugenics', the new science. The path to the *Eileithyia* Cave, the birthplace, shelter from the bombing, was stony. Looking back from deep inside, the cave mouth framed a bright blue sky. Further still was the wall of a chamber. Her fingers touched rough limestone. Deeper in, time wound back... before Clem, before even Leo, to when Easter's fate was sealed.

The old rope swing creaked as the branch moved out over the water with each thrust of her body. She leaned back and let her long hair dangle so that it swept the surface of the river. She could swim but not in this. They had all been warned about the speed of the West Allen below Staward Peel. Only in the deep pools did it slow and lie low for a while. Easter Garnet was to marry her earnest cousin, Ephraim... What did the Bible have to say about cousins marrying she wondered? But there was no stopping it. Their fathers had decided, so it would have to be.

She dangled in the possibility of an easy slip into the torrent below, but there was the child to think about. She had thought of pennyroyal or drowning it in hot water, but she loved it already, even though she knew they would take it from her. Cecil would be sent away to America and no-one was to speak of what he had done, as though his rough arms pinning her down in the dark was her own fault; a temptress with her long, barley-coloured hair. Ephraim had already let her know for sure that the badness was on her side of the family.

She felt some pity for Ephraim; forced down the pits at twelve and only escaping at thirteen with tuberculosis. After the Great War pacifists like him couldn't get work and his family couldn't afford for him to study, despite the scholarship. The village boys had told her about the tarring, too; ambushed on his way to Bible class. His clothes were found washed up against rocks in the river, but the police investigation found nothing.

Above the sound of the creaking swing was a dripping... water dripping... a regular beat like the ticking of a clock...

The Empire Clock in the best room ticked. There were coals in the grate and the fire was made up in case they had visitors but it was not lit. Clem shivered slightly.

Ephraim, in shirt sleeves, braces and armbands said, "There's no help for it. You've inherited the bad blood from your mother's side..."

Silence hung in the room. "If I had not been forced to marry into her side, I might have improved the strain. Blood will always impede you. You must struggle twice as hard." He brought his face close to Clem's, "We are on the edge. A pauper family has no merit." He lowered the sloping top of the desk and produced a sheaf of squared sheets of paper covered with figures. "Do you know what these are?" Clem was silent.

"These are my accounts for the Toy Shop. It is going down hill. As I have taught you, we can help the poor but in the end if they don't help themselves pauperism is deserved. For us

71

poverty would be a punishment for the sins of the forefathers."

"Why did you marry my mother?" asked Clem.

His father's face darkened. A fly buzzed at the window. Ephraim grasped his copy of the *Newcastle Evening Chronicle.* "Before your thoughts turn to marriage, consider the stock," he said. "It is in your power to strengthen weakness with virtue. Do it for the sake of your unborn progeny."

As he spoke he lifted the newspaper and brought it down against the window pane, swatting the fly with a quick neat blow. "There is something else I must say to you. When your papers come you must be ready to stand before The Tribunal and do as I did in the last war. You must state conscience as your objection to the call-up. Be prepared. Start writing your plea."

Leo was already flying a *Hurricane* and Reuben was at the front. His father would not countenance any talk of the RAF.

"I've been thinking about it…" ventured Clem

"There is nothing to think about. You must show strength of character now. Use your good blood to fight against the bad."

"I don't think I understand. What has good blood to do with this? It is surely a matter of conscience".

"I am afraid for you it is more than this," said his father.

November

Lou

If she was quick, the teacher had the chance of ten minutes in the pool before the session while her class was supervised in the changing rooms by attendants. Lou's toes curled as she dipped them. Deep breath. Gingerly she slithered down the side of the pool, let go, plunged and broke surface, breath knocked out of her with the shock of cold. At first she doggy-paddled, then, as her body warmed, drifted. In her ears were winds through spiral shells and fizzing kettles. Over onto her belly, breast-stroking the water, water stroking her body, sides and thighs... tile floor broken into a shaky mosaic.

Clem Renshaw was a dark horse. She turned over onto her back and floated again, water splaying her hair like a sea anemone in a rock-pool. The water felt warmer now. She trailed her arms; vision blurred, diminished by this space. If she ever... became close... to a man she would tell him her story in good time.

She scissored her legs and arms and spread them star-like, in the thickness of water, a spider suspended in amber. Pain at the back of her nostrils. Points of light above. Break surface. Sounds bounced about as she got her bearings. The class was coming in. She breast-stroked to the ladder, towards flecks of light jumping on the walls. She broke and broke them again, ruffling the surface...

...clouds leaden in one direction and aluminium in the other. She preferred the lead. There would probably be a shower before they had time to finish. They stretched out on the slatted wooden seat of one of the cliff shelters. Lou folded her leg and rubbed at an old patch of gravy browning on her calf.

Her father seemed tired at the moment. There was no peace and quiet to write his sermons. And he was losing sleep thinking he should be on the front line, trusting to God and ministering to the troops. She had heard him talking to Cyril Moon about it; how he wanted to give himself, felt so keenly the guilt of being out of it, prayed for his vocation to be revealed. She would quietly sneak the gravy browning back into the scullery and hide the eye pencil under her knickers tonight.

"You can do my seam now, Fern," said Lou. She lay along the slatted bench, legs bent at the knee, picking at a flake of

74

green paint. Most of the paint had cracked off the seats and on dry days they were bleached the colour of driftwood. Fern knelt beside her. She licked the eye stick. Lou had found it years ago in a lacquered make up box someone had dropped. It was vanity to use it, so she kept it secret, lacerating the pages of *A Good Child's Companion* with her father's penknife to make a hiding place.

Fern's lines didn't wobble the way her's sometimes did. Now, though, she spat on the corner of the hanky and rubbed at Lou's leg.

"You know," said Lou, "my father told me the other day he has a cousin who emigrated to Italy and is making a name for himself as a sculptor there." She scraped at the paint. "He's called Nathan Copperwhite. No-one ever mentioned him before... except without really speaking outright... because of him being a black sheep."

"What kind of black sheep?"

"I'm not sure exactly – family secret. Art can lead to wickedness, of course... with it being a bit papist. Besides, Mission angels don't have real bodies. It's more convenient that way... otherwise the devil might tempt an artist with ungodly thoughts about the models for his seraphim."

Fern laughed.

"Anyway he didn't go in for the Mission and lived like a Bohemian in London and Paris before going to Italy. He lives in sin, I think."

"What made your father tell you now?"

75

"I think he may know about the stocking stain and seams. I was lax with the gravy browning and he saw it on my bedside table when he came up to say prayers with me one evening. He didn't say anything at the time but made a remark yesterday, as though he was talking to himself, "What a great pity nice young women fall for painting themselves when the Lord made us all as he wanted us to be. How can we better his works?""

"Did he say what the consequence of trying to improve on creation might be?"

"He believes you shouldn't rush to cast a stone. You should try to help if the person is in trouble. Anyone... even your daughter might one day need saving."

"Anyway I think it sounds jolly being a sculptor." Fern drew the eyebrow pencil down the seam line with just the right pressure, so there were no flaky bits this time. She measured it just above the skirt length, above the knee. It was best not to crouch too much in case it smudged.

"All we need now is a tulle skirt instead of *Butterick* patterns made up from old clothes unpicked," she sighed.

Clem

Most of the model planes were stored on a shelf here in Ida's outhouse. He noticed as he sorted out stuff for the jumble and bits of wood for model-making that they were looking rather shabby now. This had been Pinck's workshop. He used to be quite handy at mending a stool or framing a picture, Ida said. Clem shivered despite the warm afternoon. The outhouse had a wooden floor that creaked and breathed like a ship's deck. A smell of pine resin filtered through the air from a stack of wood to one side of the door. He turned over one or two pieces. Alongside the firewood were some old bookshelves. He would take those.

The place was piled with salvage from other times, things Ida held onto to remind her. There was a brown cloth trunk with wrinkled leather bindings and two fire screens, a collage of valentine hearts and primroses just discernible under yellowish cracked lacquer. Two tea chests were still being used as storage and at the bottom of one was a mass of old odds and ends of wood. He tipped it, reached in and was engulfed in a rich fruit-wood smell. A dark-green wave of memory surged... scavengers - desperate German children. Clem forced himself to count the oranges on an orange tree tea set, more delicate and less serviceable than Ida's everyday one, but the images persisted... scrawny, dirty children with empty bellies. The ransacked grocery store reeked of tannin and metallic blood. A sack spilled dark tea mingled with the blood leaking from a corpse. The one with the gun had used it accurately.

He forced himself to focus on the task. He could shift that old butcher's bike, half covered with a sheet, to make some space. He turned his attention to the other chest which was stacked with books; a copy of *Tom Brown's Schooldays*, a dedication on the flyleaf — 'W. Driffield, Christmas, 1904' and a sketch of a fat Saint Nicholas in green and red inks. He lifted the lid of the trunk. It was bursting with photograph albums and scrapbooks of news cuttings. A pressed flower dropped from its pages and the line, 'Hamburg wiped off the map by air raid' jumped out at him. And there was a photograph of Lancaster bombers in flight, dated August 3rd, 1943, only a few weeks after his call-up... the day before his Tribunal.

On the same day, his sister Isabelle made her declaration of love for Cousin Leo, vowed she would marry him. It all came out then: an impossible love. Leo was not their cousin. Ephraim pronounced that they were all tainted by Easter's fall, that Leo should never set foot in their home again. His mother cried, tears bubbling by the ash-pit; refused to come into the house, even when it got cold. Clem put her shawl around her shoulders and stood with her while his father and Isabelle held long conferences in the Best Room.

His mother was different after that – slumped. She buried her light-hearted side, the side his father called giddy and said needed chastising out of her, the side that sang old songs her own father taught her. The young teacher from the girl's school, Lou Rainbird, came to mind suddenly. She reminded him of his mother. Her natural laughter, the way she could see the funny side.

Clem flipped over a few leaves and there it was... the news photograph he had avoided when rifling through his father's box of war cuttings. Cameras whirred even as they opened the gates of *Buchenwald* and *Belsen*. Underneath was scribbled in pencil, 'God's creation?' He snapped the book closed too late... the man's bulbous eyes in brown sockets, glazed fish eyes, watching and waiting. He wrenched himself back. Time to get the job done.

Ida was right; it was time to start afresh. Clearing out the planes would kill two birds with one stone; make a space so he could move on. Deliberately, he lowered the *Dakota* into the bottom of an apple crate. The *Liberator* would need more newspaper to protect its turrets, bristling with guns. He lifted it to eye level and inspected the carefully detailed, bomb-shaped mission marks. The pin up of Athene on the nose cone was a humorous touch; Americans went in for comic book style. He had debated whether to call it 'Pacific Princess' or 'Bathing Belle'. He grasped the *Spitfire* and curved it in a series of arcs and loops imagining Leo, a damsel fly darting.

At the back of the shelf were some of his architecture books, the ones he had rebound himself after discovering his father's bookbinding press under a frayed overcoat in the shed. They lay slumped against the tool box. He lifted the lid: a wooden folding stick, its curlew design carved with a penknife, the plough for cutting the pages, hammers, brushes, sieve and sponge. Further down were straw boards, calico, cord, leather and end papers in dark marbled blue. The marbling trough was under the table, the bloodstone nestling in it. He slipped the green chalcedony with its smears of bloody red into his pocket as a talisman.

The Mission Hall was a temporary building between the Aero and the Jigsaw Puzzle Club cabins, all hastily erected after the bombing. Inside was a foyer with song books piled on bookcases. Notices, duty lists and requests for household items needed by families struggling to rebuild were tin-tacked to a board. In the main hall tables were set out and heaped with donated bed linen and winter clothes. He could hear clattering cups and chit-chat coming from a little room at the back.

As he glanced round for a space on one of the tables he caught a flash of an emerald green wool skirt; someone was rummaging behind one of the tables. A young woman stood up.

"Clem Renshaw," she smiled, "Sorry. I didn't hear you."

It was Lou Rainbird. She eyed the crate Clem was carrying. He felt foolishly self-conscious carrying a muddle of old toys.

"I'm not sure why I kept these," he said. "You hang onto some odd things don't you?"

"I was inconsolable when my mother gave mine to the rag-and-bone man." She pointed. "There's space on the end of this table."

He clutched the bloodstone in the well of his palm. One day he might use it once more for polishing a gilded edge. Automatically, he laid it on the table.

"A semiprecious stone? What is it?" asked Lou.

"It's called a chalcedony, bloodstone."

He lowered his crate onto the trestle and reached for the book closest to hand, Gibbon, *The Rise and Fall of the Roman Empire*. The bindings had split and the cloth cover came away at one side as he examined it. A cut with the plough needed precision and rounding with a hammer. It was a delicate operation. He unloaded each item carefully.

The volunteers appeared from the back room and presently a trickle of buyers became a small crowd. Two little boys came and stood in front of his part of the stall. Clem handed the smaller boy the *Hurricane* and his brother the *Spitfire*. The younger one took the plane and held it up, grinning, but the elder boy shook his head.

81

"I don't want any money for them," said Clem, "Just a good home. Someone who appreciates aircraft engineering," he continued, sizing up the older boy. The boy looked solemn, considering the proposition, then carefully extended his arm. "Of course," said Clem, "let's shake on it." He took the boy's hand and they shook hands, formalizing the deal. Clem handed the *Spitfire* over and the boys ran off. How foolish that he had hung onto the planes for so long.

"They'll remember the man who unexpectedly gave them a present," Lou whispered.

"Let's hope they have a childhood," he said.

"We survived didn't we – just about."

That evening Clem lay on his bed. The flights were becoming part of his life. Sometimes vague memories would linger and afterwards he was exhausted. He glimpsed the painted metal globe in the corner of his room as he rose. He followed the coastline for a while. Further out to sea grey battleships were shuttling men who looked towards the horizon. The sea changed from metallic to green, pale and flecked as a dish of mint jelly…

Raven

Raven perched on the ledge at the mouth of a Cretan cave. She squawked, her head slightly lowered and thrust forward for full throttle. She raised her head and stood upright, scratching her cere, then roused, ruffling her feathers. Behind her she felt vibrations from the cave; dripping, scratching, soft breathing. They blew around the arches in her skull. Her bird-memory was wordless and without thought, another kind of knowing. The shawl of feathers at her nape had become capillaries for blood at the quill as her beams and flags lengthened. She spiralled through time, her alula growing to direct and brake her flight, all the little bones dividing and slotting into place as she flew.

Sometimes the cave shivered with human wails and belly sounds; rhythmic shuffles would shake her out of dreams. In her memory was a trace of tree and sky framed by the bark hood of a cradle, the wind tossing and a croak of laughter.

The storm from the south would reach here shortly, but high on the mountainside she was disconnected, with a raven's view spread below her. She huddled into her feathers and made her way down towards her workshop.

Creation. She watched them emerge as she split rocks. They hatched with stray shavings of shale or sand clinging in their fluted fins or spinal columns. There were feathered ground dwellers with a wing stretch the span of a bridge and others, crouched in anticipation of the articulation of bones, always about to rise, but silted and stilled in that instant. She sculpted as though working in reverse, a backward glance at those petrified in limestone.

Ravamanthys' dark eyes glinted, motioning Clem towards another cavern. As she entered the sculptor's workshop, Raven lifted a lamp so that it gleamed around the hollows of her work. It was slow going; a slip with the chisel might sheer away bone that should protrude. No twitching muscle could be restored once fractured. Raven scrutinized the grain and flaws in the rock before she made a single knock or opened a crack. She hacked and chipped out her best work in darkness, feeling along fissures and hair-lines, her fingertips sensitive to each swell and scoop and to the imperceptible shifting of plates on a molten, volcanic sea.

"This place is a fracture zone. The floor, straddling a deep rift between limestone and dolomite, may shift beneath us at any moment." she said.

A brow of wrinkled hide and bulging eyes was emerging in monstrous relief from the rock face. From the side of the head curved a tapering horn cradled by the cranial overhang.

"They wear away faster than they grow," said Rhavamanthys, her eye glinting.

Clem lifted her hand to touch the stone nostrils, slippery with the fluids that moistened the rock. She felt hot breath on her cheek as the head lowered and the eyes rolled.

Rhavamanthys laughed, a deep belly laugh, and Clem saw that the sculptor's head was covered in dark feather-like curls. There was an avian gleam in her black-blue eye as she swung the lamp again, leaning over to set it on the ground. Hammers and chisels were strewn on the ground as well as axeheads, a shaft to slot them into, a pick, a series of metal wedges of different sizes, some stones and a bucket of sand. Against the wall was another jumble of things: an artists easel, pencils, charcoals, pastels, tubes of paint, set squares and a jointed folding ruler with brass hinges and deeply incised measure marks. The half circular pivot ruler was like Ephraim's, still marked with the stain a spilt pot of black ink left. Rhavamanthys weighed a chisel in her palm.

"The creature is almost breathing," said Clem. She could hear what sounded like human voices, but distant, setting up strange harmonies. What would a child hear in the womb? She saw Easter's face, the familiar creases around her eyes as she pinched and patted, singing her people's songs.

85

Rhavamanthys straightened up. "Ah, that takes work – learning from your rock – the surface and its interior, its composition, what it wants to give you. This is what the Nazi artists couldn't understand with their desire to curb rather than coax. They beat me with rifle butts when I said it wasn't possible to bring their eagle from the rock, but they knew they couldn't get what they wanted. The oppressed always have some freedom in reserve that can't be reached."

Clem stretched out a hand to touch the bull's flank. Her skin prickled. She traced the shape of the triangular frame of bone at the rump, the 'huggins', and drew her finger along the pins protruding on either side, the tail slung between them. She squashed her fist into the knotted muscle above the forelegs. It twitched and for another moment became the musculature of a man. A snort became a bellow. Rock strained and whined as sinew and muscle tensed hard and stone cracked open.

It was a wrench to pick up the easel and scattered pencils and paints and follow the lumbering bull upward and out towards the light, even though she knew, as Hitler's artist, that this was her task. Night was withdrawing but the sun had not yet shredded the haze. The bull stood blinking, its long lashes framing sulphur yellow eyes. The footpath from the cave was steep with an overhanging brow of hill above them. The bull snorted again and pawed the ground, one hoof uncloven where it had broken away before Ravamanthys finished the detail. Above the cave entrance a triangular rock jutted out like a beak. Raven gripped a finger-like spar and croaked, a coarse laugh rising on the air.

Clem grasped tufts of coarse hair and mounted the bull's back. Dusted with crumbled grains of shale it paused to test this new weight then began to move heavily. Clem felt for the hide swaying in hoops from the neck. They rocked down a stony track where lizards darted from each hoof-fall. Olives grasped crannies, grown into fantastical shapes as they leaned away from the wind. The bull paused under a parched fig tree then lumbered over scree, the scent from stunted lemons drenching the air.

At the ruins of Knossos a naked soldier was seated on a low wall. She had seen that face before. The parachutist who later raised his gun to the child. Clem glanced at the book that lay open near him on the rock; an illustration of St. Michael wreathed in the coils of a serpent, sinking his sword deep into its flesh.

The Artist sent by Hitler to Crete was to come to Knossos and Otto was ready. He would pose as Hitler the bull slayer, heroic, pitted against the beast of chaos. He touched his moustache and flipped the page of the book. 'The word in stone' was how the *Führer* described ancient architecture; proportion, health, natural beauty. The Nazi Emporer would be immortalized, captured as though in one of Arno Brecker's sculptures. The *Führer's* rhetoric filled his mind. Only the warped mind painted a sky green; such a person should be sterilized. The end of *entartete kunst;* the death of decadent art.

With self-discipline he could train his own mind... one day he might kill his brother for Hitler, even though his father loved only Günther, his half-brother.

He raised his head to the ruins and faced the monstrous bull, the glossy haunches and steaming muzzle. He was filled with a wild excitement. A woman was setting up her easel; Hitler's official artist. Of course, they had chosen a woman for the task.

Clem held up her finger vertically and squinted as she aligned it to the perpendicular of a ruined wall. She screwed up her eye and took sightings of the distances, calculating proportion and perspective. After a few moments she began to sketch rapidly, the rippling hide, the heavy folds around the neck. She must capture the weighty substance of it, the solidity of form and stance. She would give the ruins a sense of menace; ancient masonry, tumbled slabs, parts of the walls still standing. Clem smudged and rubbed to achieve the precise texture of the coat. She stroked the page with a softer pencil; shadow here would point up the light. The animal seemed to be moving under its own skin, gathering itself together.

Otto shivered. He noticed for the first time the dark clouds piling up to the south. A handful of low slanting beams of early sun struck the back of the beast that stood facing him, only yards away. The ropes of hide hanging from the creature's neck seemed to harden into stone, creases in its hide etched out by shadow.

Clem worked to make the image glorious. The sky must be gold around the sun and, behind Hitler, shot through with perfect columns of light. The boy was beautiful, pure skin for her to borrow; her painting the lens through which Hitler would bend minds to his vision.

Without warning Otto roared and pounded forward, bare feet kicking up stone-dust, his pike supported by both hands. Clem would capture this moment, the youth pliable as a sapling. The beast snorted, nose toward the ground, eyes raised, back tense. The boy drove his pike into the soft earth, piercing the ground, and vaulted forward towards a perfect landing on the bull's back.

Otto stood triumphant for one moment, proof that he was not merely a piece – Jews were *stüke*, pieces – but he the whole, the glorious whole. He held his pose, suspended there, until the enraged bull sprang from its back legs, catapulting its load upwards, lowering its head. Its horn, poised, snagged, then gored his soft tissue. Blood dripped from his wounds, darkening the dust and crusting brown in the sun.

The bull turned and ambled back towards Ravamanthys' cave, the scent of fennel and aniseed wafting as its hooves crushed leaves.

In the ruins Ephraim shuffled in his leather slippers, the backs worn flat, head bowed and muttering. It had all spilled out accidentally, as it was bound to do. Leo was to visit. Easter was happy, liking to see the boys together, until Isabelle made her announcement. Ephraim inflated with fury. Easter was silent.

"I thought you would be glad for me," Isabelle cried.

Ephraim shook with rage. "Leo is no cousin. Leo is your half-brother. Leo is your mother's son."

A voice spoke over Clem's shoulder; "Your father told you in the end, brother."

As he returned from his flight, the roofs and gardens came into view with their straggle of potting sheds and the fields beyond where the fox yarled its mating call. Closer in, he could see the blackcurrant canes and the painted eye of the flaking green plaster crocodile. As his eyes adjusted, he focused on the scattered pages of letters strewn about his bed. There was the bloodstone. He opened his palm. The stone fitted snugly in the hollow, hot and smooth and thicker than water.

December

Lou

Cold burned her ears and throat. Before long there would be icicles in the eaves and a frosting on the tramp's beard – an old soldier, most likely. If her father had still been in the Mission he would have set up a 'Returner's Cadre' for the ones whose families had disowned them. He would keep them from being found poisoned by alcohol in seaside lodgings.

She tugged her old brown school beret further down over her ears and her scarf up to meet it. As she rounded the corner of the bike shed she caught sight of Clem in his flying cap, smoke curling round his ears. She thought about him at odd times. Sometimes his motorbike was in the shed when she arrived, sometimes not. She braked, jumped off and pried at the ropes tying her satchel to the bike, her fingers raw and stiff.

"Can I help you with that?" Clem peered at the knots as though they were of real interest. "I like to practice my unbinding skills – in case I'm ever shipwrecked."

He unravelled the clove hitches and freed the satchel from the carrier.

Lou produced a paper bag from the little case that hung behind the saddle. There was a tearing sound and a blizzard of feathers drifted into an icy puddle. Clem opened his canvas knapsack, fished about and fetched out a drawstring shoe-bag, scattering some small blocks of wood. He pushed the sandshoes back into his knapsack and began scooping up feathers and shovelling them into the bag.

"Look here's a robin's feather." Clem held up a reddish feather with downy fronds that stirred in the breeze.

Lou laughed. "I'll dry them on the classroom stove. We're doing some stuff on flight." She bent down, picked up some small blocks of wood and handed them to him.

"Model making equipment – Roman Army camps." he explained.

"I'm glad you do that sort of thing. Rather than nothing but reading and writing."

Clem scratched his ear. "How do you find the girls' school?"

"Exhausting. There's Daphne who bangs her desk lid down on purpose. Then her partner gives her a shove to stop her. That just makes her bang louder. What about you?"

"Much the same. I'm sharing a classroom with Colin Silcot who lost his leg in the war – as a Bevan boy – got trapped in a rock fall down the mine. He keeps reminding me the Bevan boys weren't pacifists; they were chosen by lot as their call-up came. Quite bitter about it."

Lou nodded, wondering where Clem had been in the war. He was probably a few years older than she. She slung the satchel onto her shoulder, only glancing back when she reached her separate entrance. What was Clem's loss? ...

...crusted snow that would hold their weight a moment then give. Icicles fringed the banks of the Kale as it threaded sand and wormed mud to bulge in blisters at the edge of the sea. Lou shivered and blew on white fingertips poking through fingerless gloves. Even the sand was crisped with frost. Her toes inside the boots were curled over with cold.

"Meek's not coming back next term." she said.

"Spark says he's a pacifist."

"Mmmn. Some of the boys call him a *Conchy* and boast that they refused to be taught history by him."

"I'd rather Meek than Marshall." Mr Marshall had come to teaching after retiring from the army. He made them tear two pages out of their text books, saying they were unpatriotic.

Lou stamped her feet. There would be a shovelful of hot coals in the bedroom grate tonight and the smell of smouldering tea leaves and peelings banked up on the fire downstairs.

"Come on shouted Fern. Race you to the museum."

It was dark early at this time of the year, so their storytelling hours were cut short. They followed the faded circle of light cast by Fern's lowered torch to the museum. In the Egyptian room they stopped to pore over the smallest mummy, its flesh shrunken, but wearing tiny bangles, its delicately creased linen bandages steeped in honey and spices.

"She's beautiful," Lou whispered. In here voices were thrown back amplified by the domed ceiling.

"Like an acrobat, the way her feet are extended or as if she's on point at ballet."

"I feel as though we're disturbing her sleep. She looks as though she could wake at any moment."

"Sleeping Beauty - asleep in a castle surrounded by thorns and briars for a hundred years."

"Until she was called by name like the poem," Fern said.

"Yeats," Lou added, quoting the lines from The Song of Wandering Aengus. She let her voice rise so that the echo juddered for a moment like an uneasy laugh.

It was dark outside and an attendant who had seemed half awake peered at them. They linked arms and made their way out through the Bronze Room with its fragments of cauldron and burial urn, pausing at the *History of Bookmaking* exhibition and the parchment scrolls made of goat skin. In the distance a

94

dimly lit tram jolted past where Land's End Street joined the prom.

"What if she woke up here now," pondered Fern, "with cities burning?"

"Endlessly having to stand in queues when she is used to wriggling her toes in the Nile."

"Not knowing whether a bomb is about to change everything forever."

The warden at the ARP booth called across at them to hurry home. As usual she was smoking and half-reading *Picture Post* while keeping an eye out. They waved and hurried on.

"I think she would be better sleeping or waking at home with papyrus leaves in her hair," continued Fern. "It's so dark here – all day long."

Clem

Today's Christmas assembly would settle the issue. After this it wouldn't only be Colin Silcot who hinted that Clem was 'The Pacifist'. Bella Corbyn, the Girl's Head, had asked him to speak at the joint assembly. Last night he'd had the recurring dream. He was in the little Methodist chapel in Pegswood where his father had lived as a boy. The scene changed and he was climbing into the roof space of the house where he had been an evacuee Grammar School boy. He opened the door onto the flat roof and found himself looking down on the patchwork of a city. Close to him on the roof, leaning against a wall, was a body wrapped in bandages. At first it looked like a tiny baby's body, but as he came closer he saw that it was much larger; the face was a man's... and the smell...

The Head was bending over him. She nodded. "We're ready for you now, Mr Renshaw."

"Oh yes, of course." he muttered.

He turned to pick up the papers wedged in the join between his seat and the next one and noticed Lou, seated further along the front row. She caught his glance and smiled encouragingly, which only worsened his anxiety. He walked towards the makeshift podium at the front, as though traversing a bridge... Suspend a chord between two fixed points and load it. An arch of the same curve would behave the same way. Had he really tested the theorem by dangling forks and spoons from Easter's washing line? He shuffled the papers and cleared his throat.

Raven

After the swim Clem stood still, scanning the lower slopes of the mountain where a line of twisted olives followed some forgotten boundary. When the surface of the pool calmed it cast back an image of a short crop and stubbled chin. It was no surprise to find himself male again. He pulled the Cretan shepherd's tunic over his head, his body heavy with heat. It was time to move on up the steep mountain path. In the opening of a cave a woman was rolling a stone and wrapping it in folds of cloth, lapping it over and over.

The mule brought him to a deserted village where almond trees grew and goats foraged among windfalls. He glanced into the recesses of a cave. There was a store of stone jars filled with offerings of oil to keep the sacred flames burning despite the Nazi strictures. Goats and sheep scrambled across the mountainside away from the cloud billowing up from below. Above him white mountains loomed in the quiet, sounds suppressed. As he arrived at the smoke-plumed village an orthodox priest and his deacon bolted in the other direction. Someone let out a throaty ululation close by. Young German boys, fuelled with drink, hollered wolf cries and set their torches to anything that would burn.

Günther was bundling a woman into a blanket when Clem found him. He lifted her onto the back of a mule and the blanket fell open, uncovering burned skin and bare scalp. Another man led the mule away. Günther, in Cretan shirt and trousers, pulled Clem into a white stone house and spoke rapidly.

"I am of the *fällschirmjager,* parachuting to spoil paradise."

The air was growing hotter and smells of burning were everywhere. He rattled opened the long drawer of a linen press and pulled from it the sketches of a new city, part drawn.

"Germans cannot object to conscription. It is fight or death. By a different route, I found myself fighting my father's war." he said as he smoothed the sheets onto the stone flagged floor, "the day I gave up architecture and became a prison guard."

The smell of burning choked the air. Günther produced the ruler with the hinged pivot and began to draw.

"Do you think our city might be built over the slope of a mountainside, full of natural wells that bubble up from the base of limestone ridges; a city of springs and waterfalls?"

"All there is left," said Clem, "Is to make houses like shells that we carry with us, travelling as refugees through the world;

houses jutting from rocks like hermit's shrines; homes clinging like snails to the top of the world where no-one can invade us and shatter our dreams; mosaic floors made from a sack of stones of broken buildings of the old world."

He sketched windowless, doorless houses and a house grafted onto the rock of a cavern.

"Beware" said Günther, "Hitler, too, claims a *revolution der gesinnung,* the mind and spirit."

As he drew forms mushroomed; bract-like roofs clung to rocks, tough as razor strop. "I thought it was possible to keep an area inside intact. My friends and I became *Scheinnazis,* Nazis only in appearance. Were we kidding ourselves? To be an architect in the *Reich* means colluding in the creation of a new mythology; massive halls with podia, everything scaled up. Etty read law. She and my other Jewish friends were not permitted to graduate. In the end, it was my brother, the artist, who betrayed us."

Still they drew; libraries camouflaged underground, the pages of books fine as the gills of fungi and museums of skulls with poems painted on their interiors floating on islands moored temporarily at lakesides.

"There will be no monuments to victory, no tall towers. We will fuse mud and steel." said Clem. From his *Richardson and Corfiato* he brought up images of mosques and minarets, domes and mausoleums and the arch of the Bridge at Kaflan Kut. "Only domes that reflect the sky or the inside of the head."

"Our roads into the interior will be laid down like a carpet and pulled up behind us."

The fire had reached the threshold of the cottage. Beams clinked and doorposts slumped, finding their level, then charred and powdered. A sudden shot of gas was released in a flare of purple, then another of green; short lived moment after millions of years trapped in a pocket.

"It is simple," said Günther. "My stepfather loves me and loathes his own son because my half brother has his father's own blend of colours. That was why Otto betrayed Etty. Any child of ours would have been *mischelinge* like him. And I've betrayed her too."

Fire cracked the trunk of a fallen cypress, stirring the embers so that a brief spurt of flame fizzled. They stood quiet for a while amid the buildings of their new city.

"And Mirrie is your child?" asked Clem, momentarily catching sight of her dancing figure balancing along a ledge of aerial homes.

"I could not let her go. She is the reason I fight for the resistance." Günther turned and shambled down the street they had created.

"I too betrayed my brother," called Clem after the retreating figure. "I became a pacifist while he plunged to his death in flames," He watched as Günther and Mirrie disappeared into the distance, a bear and a thought child.

Spring Term, 1950

Raven and the house with no door

January

Lou

Feathery flecks grazed Lou's cheek as she pedalled along the promenade on the first day of the winter term. Someone overhead was shaking out a feather mattress, as her mother would say. There had been snow on New Year's morning too as Fern's baby arrived from far away while her father travelled further from their reach. His gaze was fainter each day, the once-strong back now bolstered against the bed-head. Fern said her baby would be a changeling long before he arrived.

"My child flown from overseas," lullabyed Fern.

"Fairy child," whispered Lou.

"What gift will you bring him, fairy godmother?"

*

Under the shelter of the bike shed roof she peered into the endless falling of soundless flakes. Snow rounded the cinders along the path and plumped out molehills across the field. Flakes clung to her scarf until her breath melted them. The snow made the world as new as it was for five-day-old almond eyes. She recognised the change of gear as Clem slowed for the school gates, the sound brisker in the frosted air. They were always the early ones. Clem cut the engine and freewheeled into the shed, his pilots' cap clotted with white fleece. He grinned at her.

"We might get sent back in this," he said, pulling off his cap. He shook it and rumpled his red hair, then grasped his steamed up specs and wiped them.

"Happy 1950," said Lou.

"And to you - a happy New Year."

She watched him undo the poppers of his jacket under the shelter of the roof and fumble for his tobacco tin. She rubbed her finger ends. They stood and looked out towards the old elms, snow lodging in their furrowed bark.

"And the newest thing… is Robin, Fern's baby."

"Oh. It's come. Good."

"A fairy… handicapped child… but she doesn't mind."

Clem took a breath.

"Don't say you're sorry. She wouldn't like it. She loves him. It wasn't his fault that his Daddy… took his own life. Nor hers. Though her mother thinks it's a punishment. Of whom or for what, I'm not sure."

Clem's cigarette glowed like his hair against the white world. Under his jacket he was wearing a rainbow jumper knit in scraps of wool of varying textures and thicknesses of strand.

"Creation is a precarious business," he mumbled, his voice furred with snow breath.

Lou thought about her recurring dream, the baby that spoke to her – Robin peeping from the windows of a strange house... watching... just as they had watched...

...the rise and fall of dark water sneaking up and down the piers of the old jetty. Between iron buttresses it breathed deeply, sucking at tattered ribbons of seaweed, a bloated and dangerous belly. Lou thought of huge fish bodies swilling ropes of weed down there, like the ones in her dream.

"And you say the bookshelves were bare?" asked Fern. "They had taken them all..."

"I got back from school, opened the front door and at the first breath the air in the house was different. I couldn't think what had changed for a moment. Like when I was small being woken up in my berth on the ship and feeling it rocking," she said. "My mother used to la-la a tune to reassure me, 'The foolish man built his house upon the sand', but we both knew the air had changed. The safe old world had vanished even as she sang, pulling my jumper over my head too hurriedly. Her mind was elsewhere and her voice didn't hide the crashing of crockery."

The boys fished, crouching along the pier, until the tide turned and rose in the gloom. It licked the underside of the boards where they stood. At the next wave the planking would become slippery and wet and they would slosh precariously back to the safety of the rocks and the fish and chip shops.

"What I remember most about that night was the space around us in the moonlight. When I crossed the gangway to the rescue ship I stepped into a space with no sides, just a stomach-turning undulation below."

Lou's dream fish surfaced again, their wide-open mouths framed by a necklace of spiny teeth.

"Do you know where you were when it happened?" asked Fern.

"I think we must have been somewhere in the Irish Sea."

Her mother and father had been posted to Belfast, then Portadown. There were quite a few Missionaries there in the early thirties.

"Ireland was their first posting as married officers. We lived on turnips and potato soup but I didn't know any different then."

Soon they would make their way back along the pier, walking as far from the edges as possible. "So that's what I think of when I look at the sea between the slats. A space with no edges and all the lights gone out and never seeing the land again."

"I was reading a story like that the other day; a creation myth that starts with darkness stretching on for ever and no

107

light. It's about Raven, a sort of Creator-God of the Arctic people. Or perhaps I'll make her a Goddess. Do you think it's all right to change things like that?"

"It wouldn't mean the same thing, but perhaps stories mean something different each time you tell them."

"And you never tell them quite the same way twice."

The sea was sloshing round the stilts, plaiting seaweed ribbons higher up as it swelled.

"Anyway, when half your world is blown up perhaps you could be forgiven for a bit of make-do-and-mend and tucking it up your own way."

"It's about the darkness before everything... open and endless like being on a ship at twilight only blacker, blind-black. A girl at Peace Camp once told it to me."

One of the fishing boys had caught an outlandish spiny angler fish. He held it up warily as it thrashed about, trying to free itself from the tight nip between thumb and forefinger; other boys clustered round.

"Raven flew on until she felt a snowflake on her wing-tip. Gradually it snowed more and more until the flakes clung together. Rolling a clump back and forth she formed a ball. When it grew too heavy she spun it along her wing and up into the air. Then she flew up and under and landed on it. She scratched till grass appeared, then trees with pigs rooting underneath, cows munching and men prowling. She called the place earth and lived on it.

Earth was in darkness. The sun had been pushed out by darkness and it found refuge in the house of an old man in the innermost of a nest of clay pots. Raven knew the old man lived with his daughter in a dwelling with no door where he guarded the sun with great care. Although she watched and watched, the old man or his daughter always left the circular building on the opposite side from Raven's vantage point. So she waited until the daughter came to collect water from the stream and transformed herself into a hemlock needle and floated into her water jar woven from reeds. The girl drank the needle and she slipped into her belly and began to grow.

Some months later the girl gave birth to a pouch of black skin with a wide yellow crack for a mouth. Raven grew fast until she was big enough to play with the clay pot in the corner of the room."

Lou lowered herself onto the boards of the pier. The water was ruffling the frill of weed just below the third yellow paint mark. She knelt to look.

"At first her grandfather refused to let her play with the pots, until one by one he gave in. In the smallest was a shining golden ball. Raven laughed and fled to the smoke hole clutching the ball which she sent spinning upwards into the sky to shine on the world.

But as she herself was disappearing into the smoke hole after the sun, her grandfather caught hold of her and beat her to a pulp. He instructed his daughter to drop the battered body into the latrine.

109

After a time she became conscious and began to reassemble herself. Her grandfather saw what was happening and shattered her into fragments again, then wrapped her in bark and threw her into the river"

The edge of the sea was darkening. From a fissure between banks of low cloud a burst of sun momentarily inflamed their edges. Out there in the skies were men; terrified. Lou and Fern trudged home.

Clem

There would be no moon or stars tonight. Clem dropped a few lumps of carbide into the base of the Lucas lamp. A chunk fell onto the snow.

"So this is where the boys found those fragments of carbide for fizzing the inkwells," smiled Lou.

"They've been sweeping up dust? They used to shove it down rat holes along our way." He poured some water from a small glass bottle onto the nuggets and lit the gas. There was a faintly vegetable smell.

Lou strapped her leather satchel onto the bike. "Do you still use your crystal radio set?"

"From time to time. For old times sake I suppose." To remind him of Belgium where he had picked up Lili's 'Jewish Resistance' broadcasts, perhaps.

"Some of the boys in my class were talking about making one. I think it's important for them to know the basics of

111

communication systems. We're at the beginning of a new world aren't we? Anyway –" she laughed, "we might need it if we're cut off in this."

"Do you want to leave your bike and I'll drop you home?"

The dregs of the sunset were tinged green, still blurting snow. Clem squeezed the starter and the engine croaked into life. Lou leapfrogged nimbly onto the pillion.

He felt her arms around his waist and her body close against him as they swung out of the school gates. The light from the Lucas was feeble. He had closed down signals to himself. The Jews' radio sets and typewriters were confiscated and it was an offence for Germans to tune to any station other than the Nazi one. Secret sets had proliferated in back bedrooms or attics.

The snow had drifted on the lane. Even in the dark there were usually landmarks. He'd kept Leo's set-up. The cat's whisker for his own was of phosphor bronze but Leo had used what was to hand; a hat-pin with a piece of India rubber as insulation. "I could lend you a couple of crystal sets for your class," he called back. But she didn't hear.

Raven

Raven flew through blackness as thick as sap, on and on until she felt a touch on the tip of her wing. She tilted her wing and something scuttered across her back. Another touch and another and the something grew heavier as Raven rolled it back and forth across her wings, balancing the weight of the snowball. She pulled away and the sphere spun, moving neither up nor down. She dived downward like a leaf on a windless day in autumn. As she fell then rose again black softened to grey. She slid onto the frozen surface, grasped ice and scratched. The work was slow. A crack of light rinsed from mauve to pink. A wind moaned and rumpled her feathers. She pissed and spat on the ground to warm it, scratching until a tuft of grass and soil appeared. The ice crust caved inward, revealing water. Raven flew upwards to watch the thaw uncover a Flemish salmon sandstone facade over a mediaeval palace. It had passed through the centuries; a militia barracks, a

Nazi interrogation centre, now an FAU billet and hospital. Someone with a splash of red hair emerged from a doorway and made his way to the fleet of ambulances standing in the yard. He huddled into his coat against the wind.

After a time thaw waters spilled across plains. Raven circled over a slash of reflected silver-brown, then traced the straight bank of a canal. The heat grew heavy and her wing feathers soaked it up. She flew down and perched on the branch of an oak tree, drawing back the hood and exposing her crumpled face. Her fingers were stiff; 'rub' and 'flex'. She remembered how she had made the words and scratched them in mud. There was the word for the milky fluid that bubbled as she sucked her mother's breast; the words for 'salt' and 'tear'; words that could sting; explosions of breath.

As the young man moved his arm up towards her Raven could see every detail of his face: the downy hairs barely visible on his upper lip, the delicate curl of thin lips that peeled away from uneven teeth and liquid eyes. For a moment he seemed to swim towards her, mouth agape like a fish, fins waving, his voice distorted as in an indoor swimming pool.

Clem watched light and shade ripple along the wall and disappear. He had seen feathers thrusting through grey skin and now, it seemed, this had been a disguise.

Raven ruffled her feather cape. She opened it to reveal a jumper knitted of bracken coloured wool. Her boots thudded onto the dirt path, talons dangling behind. She dragged her beak over the top of her head, shaking out long ropes of white hair and letting the beak swing over her back, still attached to the cape.

Clem remembered a laughing woman in a long boots; Nazi paratroopers suspended from parachutes; a rowing boat on a calm sea and crawling through a cave on hands and knees, ahead, someone just out of reach.

After a time they arrived at a flagged square, sun soaking the pavement. Men of all ages stood around in huddles. A lizard scuttled along the curb stones at the edge of the church, ran into a crack and away. A bearded man, his jacket torn, was pushing a handcart unsteadily over a pile of rubble.

He muttered. "Liberated they say. A crop of Flemish potatoes from good soil rotting here. Apples – sacks of them."

Clem looked into the pile and saw rats gnawing at the contents of a sack; apples and bones.

"I am looking for my brother," he called out, "There must be an official who can help me."

"The town hall is that way," the man said, "if it's still standing."

Jeeps full of soldiers rumbled by and Clem caught the eye of a soldier in a wagon as it jerked to a halt.

The Library and Museum were decorated with a parade of muses garlanded with foliage. There was a plate just like it in Richardson. One day he might find Leo again, standing in front of a row of monumental columns, shading his eyes to get the line of sight. The geometry of the city was blown apart.

The Cathedral yard was empty. Raven, cut off from the language of sky, checked the escape route as they entered. Everywhere there were traces of his brother. Each time they paused they caught a glimpse of the back of someone as a crowd surged towards a door.

An hour before sunset they glimpsed a geometric green dome. When they reached it they saw that two of the outer sheets of copper had sheered off its octagonal surface. One brown brick side had been blasted away to expose an interior where a group of men were seated or standing beside deeply engraved pillars. Two men examined the breach in the synagogue's wall. The two slid inside. Red fabric covered the lectern. On a table beside it was a nine-branched candelabrum. A roofed box was outlined in the dusky light. A male voice began intoning a chant that reverberated deep in his ribcage and throat.

A sound like a whinny cut through the singing. Clem turned and set eyes on a woman, head thrown back, her face twisted with laughter.

"I know they are here and we will coax them out... their stories..."

A man handed her a sheaf of papers. She glanced at them and slid them into her basket.

"...bring themselves to speak... collaborators most of all..."

It was Lili's habit to take note of people without looking directly at them. She had noticed the two refugees blown in by the wind; a young man, barely a man, eighteen or nineteen perhaps, and a woman, much older, long white hair spilling over a feathered hood. Nothing was remarkable in this upside-down world.

Raven's mind filled with the things Lili knew: her father, wrenched from an airy library to be thrust into a dirt pit, a hole in his side. She wrapped her cape around her, fitted her beak, stretched her muscles and beat her wings. Her blood surged. She rose and hung above the street before flying eastward. Below, armies of buildings were shuffling or tumbling in the twilight.

Lili lifted the basket of rye flour, lentils and the remaining leaflets. Clem glanced at the one she handed him. *A German Deserter's story.* He looked up.

"Are you lost?" asked Lili.

"I am looking for the Quakers – and my brother." replied Clem.

Margarethe Reynard, with whom she had been living as a daughter, was a Quaker. Her daughter, Ilse, had been taken to a forced labour camp for sheltering Jews. Margarethe knew the English Quakers.

"I could take you there tomorrow, but its getting dark now. Come home with me tonight." She moved aside the woven cover from her basket and took out a bundle of leaflets, "Here. Distribute these as you go."

Clem followed. Lili set off at a jaunty pace, head held high, alert. She trotted down a hill of narrow sloping streets, the heels of her boots clicking. Now and then she paused to pass a leaflet to someone who sifted a mound for traces of past life. Clem followed trails and plank bridges through shattered masonry. Lili waited for him to catch up on the corner of a main street. The stench of putrefaction was stronger here. People clutching piles of books under their arms hurried out of a classical building, partly destroyed.

"The Library was hit three months back," said Lili, "They are moving the remaining books."

Clem scanned a bas-relief of 'Wisdom' and 'Justice.'

Near the docks, Lili pushed open a door into a covered passage between two tall houses. An electric bulb draped with cobwebs tinged the tunnel with strained yellow light. Clem was light-headed with hunger. The door to the house was in darkness. Once inside they climbed the staircase past long windows still hung with heavy blanket, outlines of furniture dimly perceptible.

On a landing at the top of the house Lili opened a door into a cupboard, "Can you climb?" she asked.

Though the cupboard was cluttered with brooms, cloths and zinc buckets, Clem lurched onto a rope ladder and swung below Lili as they clambered through a loft opening and into a dim space under the eaves.

He caught a whiff of something sweet and woody that reminded him of his father's desk. As he straightened up he blundered into piles of books and papers. Lili lit two oil lamps near the centre of the room and the smell of warm oil and paper blended with soot and ink. In the centre of the room were a workmanlike trestle table and a couple of chairs. The room was warm and a red stove light glowed as Lili opened the glass front to pack it with logs.

"We can light the stove even if there is no other fire in the house now. And I don't pull the ladder up after me any longer," she said.

As Clem's eyes adjusted he took in a room that was part workshop, part living quarters. Shelves built into the roof space were stacked with small wooden boxes. Lili, watching him, took one down and opened the lid, bringing it into the light. It was a case of tiny, individual metal blocks; each lettered and sorted into a variety of scripts. Lili carried the lamp over to a pedestal and drew back a mulberry curtain to reveal the printing press.

"It's a flatbed with one cylinder – good for our purposes. I work the treadle myself but there are others who help."

Her work would be different now that reports on positions of German radar were not needed. Instead of intelligence data they would tell the survivors' stories.

"Have you seen one before?" she asked.

"Only on a photographic plate," replied Clem. "As an amateur bookbinder I have always been interested, though. Would this be...?"

She pointed out the parts as she demonstrated how it worked.

"Come - you look famished." She took Clem's hand and led him to the table. She shifted some piles of books and laid a worn linen cloth along the trestle, smoothing out the folds. She had baked a loaf today and there was an egg. There had never been too little to offer the *Challah* to friends. She would feed whoever came. She placed the lamp inside the clay pot, a concession to Shabbat in hard times, and filled two bowls with a soup of cabbage and beetroot. As they ate they listened to the creaks of the old weaver's house. The stove burnt lower and chill crept through the attic.

"I failed you," said Clem. "As a pacifist."

"My father, too, was a pacifist," said Lili. "Perhaps that's why he stayed in Hamburg until he was shot. And he believed Portugal would protect the *Sephardin* there – that an agreement could be made with the Nazis."

Lili pushed a plate of chopped egg and some braided bread towards Clem. A picture hung crookedly on the wall behind her; Christ on the cross wearing a scarf. Lili intercepted his gaze. "Chagall." she said. "The Christ figure is wearing a Jewish prayer shawl. Who we are is not as simple as the Nazis would have us believe. For a long time I too lived in disguise, even from myself. Perhaps that was why..." She trailed off.

"When I was a child I did not know who I really was. '*Marrano*' they called us in Portugal – Jews forced to go underground during the Inquisition, outwardly converted to Catholicism. Our Judaism was secret. My mother taught me the habit of hiding the Shabbat lamp inside a clay pot. I did not know then that we were Jews… As Otto in Hamburg did not know, but for a different reason."

"Otto?" asked Clem. Through the shadows it seemed that there was someone else sitting at the table, smoke from his cigarette wreathing his head.

After a time Lili guided Clem towards a couch and set about simmering some coffee on the range.

She handed him a steaming beaker. "Acorn and barley."

The surface of the hot milk quickly formed a skin.

Clem felt his tongue loosen. "Pacifism is a choice not a tribe and yet I feel I am supposed to inherit it from my father. I need to know that I am choosing it," he said.

"There are things that you chose and things you inherit. I want to be of the history of my people, yet for it not to claim me utterly."

The young man sitting at the table buried his head in his hands.

"Otto did not know whether he could be both a Jew and a not a Jew. His identity too had been hidden," she continued. "And to Jews he was not one of them because the connection was through his father only. On the other hand, indoctrination told him that there was dirt flowing through his veins. Otto

121

betrayed his brother and then found he had betrayed himself. You are troubled because you have not buried your brother. Do you know the story of the first grave?"

"No." said Clem, "Tell me."

Lili began. "It is a Polish story. Adam and Eve looked at the body of their son Abel who had been killed by their other son Cain. A young raven fell from the nest and died. The old mother raven flew down and scratched a hole in the ground with her claws. She laid her unfledged offspring in there. Adam and Eve imitated the bird, making a hole and laying their son Abel's body in it. This was the first human grave."

Lili rose and led him out of a small door onto a flat part of the roof. A bulky form leaned against the wall, covered with a blanket. She pulled back the blanket to expose a parchment face, skin drained of blood, eyelids drawn down.

"His full name is Otto Vogelweide," she said quietly. "I have his papers. He is from Hamburg very close to where my family had lived since we moved there from Portugal. I was distantly acquainted with his brother through a friend of a friend, Etty Edelman." She took Clem's arm and led him back to the table. "I will tell you his story." she said.

"It was late. I was hurrying back from a meeting of the *Committee de Defense des Juifs* in the cellar of a part bombed house on Franklemon Street. As I passed a figure emerged from the gloom. He was wearing a torn jacket. It fell open to reveal severe wounds to his side and stomach. His coat was civilian but his shirt was of the type that a German officer of lower rank wears. I quickened my pace.

"He ran in front of me and fell on his knees. 'Pity me,' he said in French. 'I ask to live long enough only to write to my sister.' Margarethe Reynard helped to care for him"

She got up from the table and rummaged in a chest drawer.

"We found this." She slid a metal tobacco box over to Clem, its wooden lid inlaid with marquetry. The design was of a bird in flight, an eagle or raven. Clem opened it. Under the lid were two deeply scored symbols: a Star of David and a swastika linked by a letter M.

"*Mischling*," she said. "The Nazi and the Jew in him were at war. He was raving. He claimed he had two types of blood in his body, driving him mad. And we found this folded inside." She took out a sheet of paper, a series of sketches of a comic matador, the little figure a good likeness of Hitler pole vaulting over the bull's back and finally gored on the points of the bull's horns.

"I was careful during this time not to go to the attic except when I was sure he was asleep. One day when he seemed to be improving slightly and was more alert he heard a sound from upstairs. Zalmen was up there operating the press. I moved to cover it up, but not quickly enough. I looked at him and he looked at me. That night we made love and afterwards I killed him."

She stood up and walked to the window, moving a corner of curtain aside and looking upwards. Turning back towards him she said, "What are your secrets Clem?"

"My mother had two sons; the bastard son fought and died for his country and the other lived, a coward. Which does she love? She loved the dead one first and now she wants the living to return to her."

They drank from one glass, sipping hot liquid that burned their tongues and throat. Lili's bed was as high as the beds of his childhood and shaped like a boat. Her breasts were big and heavy, as full as though she had given birth. Clem sucked and the milk leaked onto the white of the bed linen.

His mother had fed him until his father had snatched him away "The milk is curdled. You will poison him."

February

Lou

Lou studied Clem as he rolled one of his thin roll-ups; tight and held in. It was difficult to get closer to him. He leant against a post of the bike shed, resting the tin on the seat of the *Hawk* so that it showed as plain as day: a swastika. Lou picked up the box, noting Clem's slight wince as she looked more closely.

"The tin belonged to a German soldier," he said after a moment. He struck a match and lit the cigarette.

There was another symbol close to the swastika. Lou studied it a second time. It was a Star of David.

"How did you come by it?" she asked.

"Oh you know – spoils of war," he said. Then he seemed to regret this reply. "No – well, actually I transported a body to the morgue."

"You stole it?" Lou bit her tongue, too late.

Clem bent down to retrieve a discarded packet, closed the tin and put it into his pocket. "Someone asked me to return it to his family," he said. "When I found his sister she wanted me to keep it."

"I see. It is a curious little thing, though," she said, "with those symbols under there, hidden like that." She searched for a way of traversing the distance between them. "Do you think things – objects that people keep – get imbued with a sense of those people?" Her father's concertina and books sprang to mind. Sometimes she thought she heard him playing at night, though she knew his fingers were too weak to press the keys…

…Twilight was coming. There had been an air raid not far away for the last two nights. The police had stolen her father's books and now he was going to prison for twelve months. Lou shivered and rubbed her spine against the smooth rock, its sheer side acting as a seat back in the amphitheatre of the bay. Fern put an arm round Lou and sighed. Cullernose Point was a good place to be away from people.

Lou pulled up her knees to her chin and hugged them. At school Albert Best had whispered that it should have been a hanging offence. Pacifists, ministers, people who were 'getting away with it' made good scapegoats.

"I listened to a pacifist speaking on the corners of Railton and Paradise yesterday," said Lou. "Someone threw a couple of eggs. A woman shouted, 'That's a waste of good rations.' He saw my uniform. Then he spoke to me. He said that I would understand that the fight for freedom is a mental fight, not a physical one."

"What did you say?" asked Fern.

"I didn't say anything. He scooted with his crate when someone shouted that the Bobby was coming."

Fern looked across the bay to the cafe on the wooden jetty. On the distant pier the glass windows of the pavilion had been shattered into a thousand pieces two nights ago, a mountain of shards.

Clem

There was an atmosphere of excitement in the City Hall as the horns and strings tuned up. Lou glanced at her programme.

"I was there on the first night's performance of Britten's *Serenade*," he told her.

It was October '43, after the tribunal. He'd been training with the Friend's Ambulance Unit for the past few months in Edinburgh, Worcestershire and London. This was his last chance... He was due to leave for France in a few days.

Lou looked at him. "I was there too. We were studying Blake and I wanted to hear the setting of *Elegy* My father took me."

"We might have passed each other in the crush, might even have sat next to each other." He took her hand, wishing he could say more. Things he had been managing not to remember had started surfacing again.

Lili had told him what Otto said. "It went clean through my hand and out the other side."

She said Otto held up a fragment of metal. Neither she nor Margarethe Reynard did anything about the body for a few days and then Clem arrived. Clem didn't betray Lili's story, he simply removed the body to the morgue where it was recorded as a suicide case. The papers went to the Friends who traced Eva. Later Clem delivered them by hand. Lili's story of the two brothers lodged in his mind. Otto had betrayed Günther knowing that it would lead to the death of his brother's fiancé

"Find his sister for me. Tell her the truth," Lili said. "If ever I get back there I will seek her out."

The lights dimmed in the City Hall and Clem was back in one of the concerts in the cellar of the Music School in Belgium... where he had come to know that there was something more than a boy screaming like a wildcat...

This ae night this ae night, This ae night and aa, Fire and selte and candlelight, and Christ receive my soul'

...as Clem cut off the boy's shoes, the feet black with trench foot, the foul smell.

He felt Lou's hand grip tight for a moment. Things were moving quickly with her. It was good, but he had a sudden image of Armstrong on that warm sunny afternoon: he had taken his uniform off, stripped down to his combinations and walked across to the single oak still standing unharmed out in no man's land. He sat with his back against the oak for a few moments, like a boy waiting for a picnic, before they picked him off.

'Fire and selte and candle light and Christ receive...' the words the same as those of that other concert...

Raven

...held at an old factory on the estuary. They hadn't advertised but word got around. Lili had washed her hair in hard soap and fixed it up in a loose bun. The hall was the ground floor of a disused warehouse. Massive iron columns supported the building above. They sat on wooden boxes covered with sacking. The windows, high up in the dark space above, were barred. Musicians were assembling; violinists adjusting their pegs and rosining their bows. Clem watched the place fill with lean faces, leaving war behind. He made his way along a row past people's knees, excusing himself, then straightened the sack at an unoccupied seat and sat down.

The music ascended as if building a complex of stairways and his mind drifted to the carved altarpiece at Hakendover. His stomach turned and his head was light, perhaps the result of living on potato soup and bread. Whenever he stopped the images assaulted him: grey faces, glazed eyes. Sometimes there would be a Northumbrian name: Hetherington, Dodd, familiar accents. Such a short time ago he sat in Literary and Philosophical Society Library, the clock ticking, attending to the dead of history, safely chronicled, dated and numbered.

Yesterday he had found the archaeological museum in his two hours off, letting the smell of books and beeswax polish engulf the foul stench that he carried with him… His *Pevsner* was in his bag, thumbed and leafed. In the mediaeval world ecclesiastical architecture was related to musical proportions. In this industrially proportioned factory the music was now constructing another building, an interior that could only be perceived from inside the network of notes.

Lili made her way towards him. She slipped into the space next to him and they clinched knuckles. With the music playing she lifted a tin out of her pocket and slipped it into his palm.

"Perhaps when you reach Germany you might find his sister."

A few rows in front Clem caught sight of an unmistakable profile: Leo. He seemed almost luminous in the papery air of the warehouse, lit by dim electric lights high above them. He was wearing his old brown overcoat and his little horn rimmed spectacles. Clem began to rise, leaving his body.

*

On one occasion he and Leo had visited the *Lit. and Phil. Library* as children. Clem pored over books on islands and continents, utopias; lands whose people were half-human with the heads of codfish. Standing on a stool, he had reached out to take down a book from the shelf and his fingers had moulded it into a softly powdering pile. Like Finn McCumhail, eternally afloat in a ship destined to crumble if it touched land, it held its shape a moment before it drifted into dust under his touch. For the first time he was conscious of mortality, of seeing himself from outside and knowing that he must, one day, die.

Now Clem looked, from above, on the rows of people. As he scanned them he recognised Ephraim, sitting head bent over a deeply scored workbench of dark wood surrounded by bottles, each containing a liquid which he carefully dropped into pipettes and spurted into narrow tubes. Long ago Leo had shown Clem a little wooden box containing the inventor's tools, the pipettes, the tubes and the inks.

"Think what may have happened if he had invented the ever-flowing pen," he said.

Moments later, Clem was alone on a hillside at dawn, the sounds of horns and woodwind separating themselves from the strings and occupying different levels of the space above, as if space itself were being sculpted by sound. Immense columns thrust up from below, extending outwards and upwards into forest trees and a canopy far above. Beeches branched into stately avenues of arches and, at each apex, leaves choked the mouths of green men figures, branches snaking from their beards and throats, thrusting open their engorged mouths. Below him a head turned to look up. A mouth grimaced; his remonstrating father.

"Even Isabelle's young man, the son of the village postmaster makes a better lay preacher than you... You've always been tongue tied."

Like a swimmer he paddled upward to rise through a swill of bubbles, his vision distorted by light refracted through water, eyes lanced with shafts of sun. Above him the surface was darkened by a shadow, a hazy outline of a plane, wings outstretched across the water... a *Lancaster Bomber*... or a raven.

Raven perched on the edge of the sheer-sided warehouse; one claw lifted and tucked in as she surveyed the moonlit city below. The light was grey and soft. Somewhere a great mistake had been made; they simulated the flight of birds only to crack buildings like walnuts and leave the shells. She watched as Clem caught his breath, clinging to a broken pediment.

Clem's gaze panned the estuary and across the seven bridges, taking in tiled roofs and stepped gables and the geometric, classical lines of the old museum. He could forget himself for a moment, gazing at elegant stone mullioned windows softened with a tracery of foliage. Yet, the front was no more than a couple of miles away. Each time he lifted a stretcher, the face could have been a friend's. The shape had been Raven's; an augur at times of disaster. Once more he observed a hand appear from among the feathers and lift off the beak as though it were a mask. Raven cocked her head on one side and regarded Clem curiously.

"You have not yet told me your story," she said.

"I don't yet know it… but it comes closer when I hear a story of someone else."

He fumbled in his pocket, unfolded a creased sheet of paper and passed Raven the series of comic sketches of the athletic Hitler and the bull.

Raven studied them carefully. Her feathers began to ripple until gradually her whole body shuddered. The shaking crescendoed, erupting like an earthquake that split the seams of her cloak. She replaced her beak and tipped her head up towards the sky.

The sky was clearing as Raven and Clem took off from the pediment of the corn exchange. The arched bow of sky was filleted leaving a herringbone tracery. Below were the cupola of the Cloth Hall and the four Gothic spikes of its tower. They flew low between the cathedral spires so that they could have touched the lead casing on the dome of the Basilica or the bronze monkey crouching on its tiny platform. A wind started

135

up, blowing across cornfields. Bearded barley was illuminated suddenly by a bright flash. Heat rose towards them as flames roared into life. The rye crop dried to a black crisp in minutes, a charred smell clawing the back of Clem's throat.

Down below a man was running along a line of plane trees, veering like a stunned animal. They closed in on him until he felt their shadows and twisted to look up. Clem recognised the dark hollows around the eyes of the German who had leaned against a roof-porch.

Lili pulled the cloth from his face, turned and smiled at him.

"He told us how he'd crawled through fields and slept in barns at night." She held out a piece of metal.

Otto climbed a fence, stumbled to the ground and began to drag himself forward. He was bleeding heavily, the blood soaking the swastika on his uniform collar. Water was running close by. Clem could at least wash away some of the blood. He lifted Otto's arm over his shoulder and clasping him, put his own arm behind the young man's knees. The undergrowth was not too dense and Otto's emaciated body was light.

Clem stumbled and Otto, jolted, opened his mouth but instead of complete words, it bubbled with blood and spittle. He was clutching a fragment of metal and now he raised it. "Base metal... Hitler... philosopher's stone... ha-ha... oh God... he thinks he is... blasphemy... like a creator... gold... the eagles feather... if he dies... Germany will die... ha-ha... immortality... empty... charlatan..."

He shook the piece of metal. And then he was lucid. "Went through me," he said, "right through – clean. Iron or gold, it makes no difference."

He leaned against Clem, the blood from his face and arm staining Clem's uniform. Easing his pierced hand inside his uniform, he produced a small tin box with a raven design in the lid. He passed it to Clem and motioned for him to open it. Inside was a letter, folded, rubbed and spattered with mud. It was addressed to 'Eva' and signed 'from her brother Otto'.

"They'll shoot me." He leant forward, close to Clem's face. "No regret. No pity."

Clem pulled the cloth away from Otto's wound to wash it. His skin was pale as fish flesh. He flinched as Clem removed the jacket. *Vulnerare* – to wound. Clem thought of his Latin, how to describe the awful mess of insides exposed. Vulnerable.

"I loved him too much… my father," said Otto. He contorted suddenly into a sitting position. An arm folded into a vice, gripping Clem by the neck, trapping his windpipe.

"Careful – I have a knife. One slit would open you up. Easy. Easy."

Clem's own knife, used for field jobs, cutting away clothing or bootlaces, was in his belt.

"And you won't try anything," Otto hissed, "Will you pacifist?" Otto spat. "I have killed Jews for no other reason than that they are Jews. You could slide your knife between my ribs. It would be an act of heroism, the best kind… unseen, *nacht und nebel,* night and fog."

Clem stayed very still. "I know you Otto... I, too, have a brother."

Slowly Otto released his grip. Clem sat up and rubbed his neck.

"Take my knife." Otto handed it to Clem "To kill me would be an act of mercy – put me out of my misery. No-one would know... *männerbund*... unless you blabbed." He closed his eyes for a moment. "Are you afraid I'd haunt your conscience? True – you wouldn't be able to let me go." He closed his eyes and seemed to sleep, but then said, "We won't slip back into the ordinary world, you and I. Few return from here."

Raven moved through smoky air, crackling with maybugs and flies. She flew over lines of trenches where one side or the other had gained the length of a field; back to the protected land, front to the enemy. As she flew a soldier took a pot shot at her. In the distance a stream of bombers took off; machines holding young pilots and crewmen, driven by fear, orders and passion. Hulls of buildings split. In the woods Clem looked up into a sky stiff with metal birds in formation. Otto was sleeping fitfully now. He had patched him up as best he could; a local farmer might be more merciful than the army in the end. Clem turned to face the city.

*

In the city a pile of rubble with jagged spurs had replaced the four towers of the Cloth Market. How would Memling depict this? Streets like these had once been his background for *Christ's Passion* and the *Mystic Marriage of St. Catherine*.

March

Lou

Spring was a time of saplings and softening soil. Lou freewheeled in the daffodil-yellow stole Aunt Beryl had given her, bulb spears standing smartly to attention on the verges. Fern's baby was sickly, struggling to suckle and her father was fading... thin and white as the snowdrops that withered like onion skins.

"Rape," she spat as she whizzed over the viaduct. Even the word was shocking. "Incarceration." She flung the word to the breeze. And still there were crocuses and daffodils in the world.

Perhaps Clem would open up like one of the new shoots. She would study psychology at Birkbeck part time; to help her understand the children and Clem too. Her mind flickered back to the Christmas concert when he had been overcome and had not given his speech. Other staff assumed he was ill, going down with end of term influenza, but Lou wasn't taken in. And had anyone else heard Colin Silcot's sharp whisper, "Look at his eyes"?

...for, if you look into a pool you can see the future in sea anemone fronds, crab stones and bladder wrack. Her grandmother had told her fortune in tealeaves. An old wives tale, but ...

"Do you think there will be a future for us, Fern?" she called, trying to catch up as Fern moved quickly over the drier, flat rocks by the silted estuary,

Fern bounded onto a rock overhanging a pool, barnacled and with a mouthful of limpets wedged into its sides. She began to declaim like Mr Herald doing Larry Olivier. He spoke this way when he read out the lead part in Shakespeare during English class.

"We will be bound for babies somewhere in it. O come ye girls for this is all your lot. Come forth ye babes all blubber-lipped, like sucking limpets crawl across our skin."

She jumped from the rock with a flourish, landing in an ungainly heap by the pool, laughing.

Lou laid out her coat and plumped down beside Fern. "I don't know whether I'll ever be able to read any of that stuff again," she said

"You will Lou. They were wrong to convict your father. Everyone who knows him respects him."

"No they don't. They don't want to catch it off him. Whatever he's got. Even Uncle Samuel, his brother, won't speak. And everyone goes silent when I walk into a room."

"No-one can stop me from seeing you. Not even my mother. And my father doesn't believe it." said Fern.

They turned onto their stomachs and dragged the pool with their fingers, watching a hermit crab scuttle into a winkle shell.

"Miss Spark tried to help. She and Miss Jewell. They asked me about things. When I said I couldn't even look at a book any more, Spark said we'd work on it together," said Lou.

The tide was coming in now, filling up the little water courses with their rippled silt banks. What if the war dragged on and on? What if one day the tide didn't turn, but just kept coming up?

"People aren't themselves," she finished. She threw a stone into the scummy foam.

"I'm going to be a spinster. No children to have to live in a world someone else made," said Fern. "I'll sit at my spinning wheel, spinning golden yarns to fill up a room in a day like Tom Tit Tot."

"I shall run away and live on an iceberg," declared Lou. Or, perhaps, she thought, she would give up, turn the other way and face it...

*

141

…and now her future was approaching with the inevitability of a tide. Lou glanced out of the window. She looked both ways. The *Hawk* was stirring the dust, coming from the direction of the Colony.

"Here he comes, Fern," she said. "Are you sure you won't accept mother's offer to baby-sit? We could all take the bus instead."

Fern tipped the little bird's head gently towards her breast as he sucked.

"Sometimes" she laughed "it feels as though this little one has a beak. No, Lou. This is your evening and a Matchless *Silver Hawk* is your chariot"

Clem's knock was light. He stood on the step holding a jacket over one arm and a bunch of daffodils in the other.

"There's a bank of them on the Colony by the remains of that brick building – what was it - a mill or something?"

She took the daffodils and he followed her into the house. "A brick works. It was a new start for the colonists. They made bricks to build their own houses."

Fern held out the arm that was not twined round Robin. "So you're the famous motorcyclist."

Lou found a vase in the sideboard. She watched as Clem bent down and touched Robin's little hand; the stubby fingers didn't curl around his. Fern put her face next to his and blew her lips at him. Robin's tongue lolled and they stared at each other.

"Would you let me hold him?" asked Clem, "Just for a moment?"

Fern passed him over. Lou held her breath as Clem held Robin against his shoulder and sat down. He propped Robin up along his arm and tickled him gently on his toes.

Fern smiled. "I want the world to be different for him..."

...the tide high, churning sand under the groynes and flushing back up the mouth of the tributary, carrying lines of foam on its back. Lou stomped on ahead. They had to move out of the house at the college on Herne Hill. It was a Mission post and her father, their great hope and rising star, had fallen. Did they really believe he was a criminal? Whether or not - nobody was prepared to defend him.

Running down sand dunes was undignified but they weren't above it. They ran until their shoes and hair were too full of sand, shouting into the wind before they rolled into a heap, gasping for breath. Their bicycles were lying on the sand. In the distance the Home Guard were practising.

They took shelter in the bowl of a sand dune, munching cream crackers and a fig roll, carefully preserved from their rations. The wind blew above them.

"There are more casualties of war than we think," said Fern

Lou thought of her mother visiting her father in prison; writing a long letter to him every day.

"I'm scared of growing up," Fern went on, "scared that I'll end up just like the rest of them."

They packed their baskets, grabbed their bicycles and wheeled them over the sand and on to the road. The silt along the banks of the stream was salted white on brown where the heat had dried the moisture. Their boots left rusty prints following the line of oyster catcher, sandpiper and plover prints. If the war went on much longer they would have to register and be sent to work in munitions factories, do their bit for the future.

Clem

"Did you ever look upside-down through your legs?" Clem asked, swinging downward so that the school lurched into view.

Lou laughed. "I expect so...when I was young on the beach with Fern." She stretched out her arms and lowered her back, keeping it straight.

Clem staggered up, then swung his torso and his arms down to bob about his feet again. For a moment the dining cabins with Toft Rise upside-down crushed the blue out of the sky. His head sluiced with blood as he rose. Bugger Colin Silcot. Now that he knew Clem was a conscientious objector he niggled at him. Yesterday when they were clearing the classroom at the end of the day he had asked, "Do you know what kind of blood runs through your veins? That's what Hitler asked the Germans. What did the German pacifists do, Renshaw, eh?"

"They resisted or compromised for the sake of saving their schools and refugees. They made bargains. In exile in Holland and Spain they still ran centres for refugees." Colin waved his hand to dismiss this.

Now Lou and Clem both rose together. "Oh. I can't breathe," Lou said.

Clem touched her arm to steady her and found himself noticing her small delicate hand with its crooked little finger. He leaned against the shed door.

"So it was your father's idea to make the world spin like that," she laughed.

"Mmm. My family used to help on a farm in Northumberland in the summer; hay making - that sort of thing. My father lined us up – me and my sisters – for instruction – something to do with going down the pit or being out of it perhaps."

"It sounds fun."

"It didn't quite feel like fun though. My father made a serious point of everything. We were supposed to learn about architecture."

"Oh well in that case..."

He watched her peel off her sweater and neatly tuck up her skirt, then swing her body downwards again, her back rising and falling very slightly. Her hair flopped back from her neck, reminding him of Winifred when she told him that she couldn't love a *Conchy*... and of someone else...

"Looking through your legs – it's as if you're looking backwards into the past," said Lou. "Like when I take the dirt track under the viaduct instead of cycling overhead to school. Then I stop and look back through. It feels as though you have passed from one world into another."

"I know what you mean," said Clem. "How about an expedition? Beat a quick retreat from school."

"Good-O. I'm all for that. We'll take a picnic."

He swung down again to join her.

They made for the viaduct; she on the Hopper and he on the old butcher's bike he had found in Ida's shed. He had prepared a flask of tea and a tin of Ida's ginger cake. Lou brought shortbread. They bumped along the old railway track for a while and then onto the bridge. The view was breathtaking, the flight of the arches springing from the valley floor beneath. They jumped off their bikes and leaned them on the brickwork wall while they climbed down the stone steps. As they scrambled down the steep side Clem glanced upwards. Rattling across bridges in the ambulance he had occasionally felt caught in a vertiginous mesh of trusses and struts. A bridge was a way over and also a frame – in wartime it could be a target.

Towards the bottom they slithered and ran. Lou flung herself on the ground at last and pulled her knees up. Clem stretched beside her. Above, the arches strode the valley in giant steps.

"Which bridges have you crossed, Clem?" asked Lou.

"That's a big question," he smiled. "Well let's see – the wrought iron bridge at Coblenz, the Plaunen bridge with its long slow arch span, the Viaur bridge which springs across a gorge… and, naturally, all of the bridges across the Tyne."

"Would you like to have designed bridges?"

He paused. "Well… Yes. You have to build a stable structure and that gives you symmetry of form." It all depended on the load the bridge was going to bear. All at once he straightened up. "Look I'll show you," he said.

He pulled his knees up and shuffled round to face her.

"If we put our toes together and clasp hands."

She looked as though she were about to burst into laughter, but pinched her lips together.

"Now lean back. There are two tensions pulling against each other. There; we are pulling together and pulling apart at the same time."

After a few moments he loosened his fingers suddenly and they both tumbled backwards spluttering with laughter. They lay there on their backs in the sun.

Then Clem sat up, took out his roll-ups and struck a match.

"You can see the sea from here. Look." The bay was an expansive curve. "I mended a book for a Dutch boy once, about thirteen. He didn't want to take his clothes off for the delousing, even though they were stiff with filth and he'd get some fresh ones." Things were never quite what you expected, even hosing people down. "When we peeled off his shirt we found another layer underneath, thick and yellow, stuck to his skin. Only it looked like pictures, drawings of sailing vessels and photographs of whalers and fishermen. He was papered with the pages of a book. It had belonged to his father. He had no idea where his father was, but he had kept the pages under his clothes like a second skin."

Lou was silent. "Come on. Let's go and find a spot under the tallest arch," she said at last.

They jumped up and walked down the slope carrying the picnic basket between them. One side of the arch was washed by light and the other by shade. Lou spread the gingham cloth half in and half out of the shade.

They were quiet for a while as they munched the ginger cake until Lou said, "We are still hiding things, the way we learned to hide them in the war..."

Raven

…While houses burned, the communal shelters were full.
There was Allied bombing ahead of the line. *Typhoons* had fired
on German tank convoys. The city was unrecognisable;
devastated again by the line of retreating Germans as they
pulled out. Sometimes the retreat and advance came so close
together that the place just freed was in danger of being hit
again by either side. Outside, people were running and
shouting. Clem stopped a man whose hair was charred.

"The bridge is down," panted the man, "no-one can cross."

The massive stone stanchions of the viaduct yawned across
the gorge. Maquilo's Toy Emporium was built in the span of
the arch by the river. A train shunting backwards shrieked, a
spurt of steam softening the edge of the stonework as if it were
dissolving. A flight of bombers slashed the sunset. From down
river a deep rumble shook Clem as he leaned against the stone
pier. He peered up at the iron cables of the industrial lift that

carried engineers to the upper level. The fuel trails of the bombers were stained with rose dregs of sunlight.

Inside Maquilo's the counters were meticulously covered with greyed lace tablecloths, sharp folds grimy with a film of dust. Clem lifted one of the lace edgings and saw a carefully worked replica of a warship in lead-painted wood with touches of blue and red for its crew. The crowd felt their way down worn steps to the basement in the dim electric light. A woman distributed candles. A grey light filtered from a door with a pane of glass at the opposite end of the room. At the bottom of the steps a man with a flatfish oval face fiddled with his tie and jotted down names in a notebook as people passed.

Two walls on the landward side were rough hewn out of the rock. Trickles of water ran over them, glazing parts of the surface so that they gleamed darkly under the dim light. When Clem's eyes had adjusted he estimated that about seventy people were crammed into the cellar on upturned crates. On the other side of the room was a short flight of steps up to the door. He crossed the room, climbed the steps and rubbed a clear patch in the steamed glass, curious to see what was outside. Opposite, across a stretch of river was the next pier and stanchion. He turned the key and opened the door. At the bottom of a short flight of steps a boat was moored to a wooden jetty. He stepped back inside.

Back in the crowd, a woman unscrewed the lid of a flask of tea. "I always have it with me – just in case," she said, taking wheezing breaths as she poured a cup and handed it to Lili.

The man with the notebook strutted about, jotting comments.

"I've made a check by sight and asked a few questions," he confided. "It's a good job I'm here. Malisse is the name; Inspector of Munitions. You can never be too careful. It's easy for prostitutes and criminals to slip in. Or other undesirables"

"You think some people should be excluded?" asked Lili.

Malisse looked confused. "It is important to keep your books tidy. It's only natural for people to prefer to remain separate."

"What are you getting at?" asked Clem.

"I know him," said the woman with the flask of tea. "He's a Nazi collaborator. Checking identities – always checking. Issuing identity cards. Munitions inspector my eye. That's a cock and bull story. Well your friends've limped out of town with their tails between their legs, my man."

A few people turned round.

"We're all collaborators. Even the Jews." said a woman in a brown headscarf. "That's the cleverest thing those thick skulls ever did. Got us all involved. There are no clean hands in here."

Malisse took out a handkerchief and wiped his brow. "I see. I see." he said, making a further note in his book.

The roar of planes was overhead. There was an explosion nearby and the lights dimmed before going out altogether. The evening light from outside hardly penetrated. Some had brought oil lamps from the shop above. They lit them and hung them on the hooks still in the ceiling. Others lit candles.

Clem recognised the illustrations identifying the contents of wooden crates in the half-light. He had seen them before - back home in his father's shop. These were the wooden toys Ephraim sold; red-painted pigs, jigging sticks, acrobats with jointed limbs and the trains made of different colours of polished wood. Ephraim would remark on the craftsmanship, examine the trundling wooden wheels, the engines with their funnels and a guard standing on the foot plate.

Malisse had been watching Clem intently. "Why are you hiding in here? A young man like you should be at the front."

"I am a Conscientious Objector," said Clem loudly and firmly. He felt an intake of breath from Malisse and others.

"Ha, a pacifist," the man looked around for his audience.

"Here's the rest of us taking our part. Myself, for example, in a reserved occupation – essential to the war effort. However, a pacifist," he spat the word out, "A paltry excuse to avoid action."

Lili looked at the man, "Did you protest when the Jews were taken away? Did you take action?"

"The Jews themselves were passive. They wished to be martyrs. Who could deny them this? I have seen them at stations quietly boarding cattle trucks."

"Some of us find ourselves in a position to resist with violence, some without" replied Lili. "There are many kinds of courage in the world."

"Some infiltrators have sneaked in here," announced Malisse loudly. "We've got a *Conchy* in here. It is important that everyone should collaborate with those in office."

People began to gather round. "What do you mean collaborate?"

Malisse looked hot. He took out his sopping handkerchief and smeared his brow. There was a rumble like a fall of stones somewhere above. An aftershock of that last bomb, thought Clem.

The woman with the flask of tea looked up. "It's easy to cast the first stone. Anyway those Quakers helped us after the last war." She rolled up the leg of the old pair of men's trousers she was wearing to inspect a gash in her leg.

"Let me clean that for you," said Clem. "I'll fetch some water from the river." The wound would need washing if it wasn't to go septic.

Eyes followed him as he walked to the door. He rubbed at the smeared dirt on the door glass. The water level was rising. Had the dam burst? The river swirled dangerously and the water was almost to the level of the top step. Downstream it would be flooding rye and beetroot fields. The boat was battering the steps, taut against the rope attached to its mooring staple.

"It's going to flood," he announced. "We must leave. The water is rising." His voice sounded muffled.

There was a shout from the other side of the room. "The doorway's blocked. There's no way back."

A child whimpered.

The dam must have been breached. Water began to seep under the door. Clem forced it open. There was a skirl as the water created cavities under the roots of a thorn growing in the packed soil below the step. A rush of scum flooded into the shop. Malisse pushed his way to the front. The floorboards at their feet darkened as water filled with muddy earth rose through the gaps. The river had silently filled the foundations while they waited for the *all clear*. Rats shivered in a long silky stream from somewhere below. It might already be too late to escape.

A broad-shouldered man pushed forward. "Form a human chain and lift people to safety on the other side of the pier. There's just enough foothold here. Jump to it," he called.

Younger, stronger men and women rapidly assembled themselves on a ledge of the stanchion, gripping iron staples. Clem stepped into the flood; his body felt like a grass stem being tugged. He clung to the anchor of the heavier men on either side of him, their hands crushing his in their grasp, concentrating on staying upright. Others began passing children across. Some stumbled but righted themselves by hanging on to the chain of people and hauling themselves up. The ground shuddered periodically as bombers blasted away to the East.

Light leached from the sky. Toys floated from the open tops of crates and disintegrated boxes or sank in their sodden packaging. A Jack-in-the-Box was whisked away on the water.

Lili was ushered forward but Malisse put his arm out to bar her way, his thin lips like the straight lines of his book. "No, no," he said, "I have a list. There are others who take priority."

Clem glanced at the doorway and saw the woman with the flask lift it and bat the man's notebook into the water. Without it he floundered, fishing for it. Lili steadied herself as she clambered into the strong current. There was always someone behind to push and someone in front to pull. Clem caught sight of the boat tipping further, nose down. The strength of the current bruised him as he clung in line. The men next to him both gripped the root of a thorn, knuckles white. He mae out a fleet of four miniature boats bobbing against the limbs of a tree that had been ripped out of the bank and stranded.

Suddenly he became aware again of Malisse. The man held up his saturated notebook and grasped Lili's arm propelling her back towards the boat. "There are judgements to be made," he shouted above the roar of water.

Clem broke the chain, forcing together the hands of the men on either side of him until their fingers locked. He ploughed back towards the cellar, hardly seeming to make progress. At the door he stumbled back into the swirling pool that had been the cellar and against Malisse, who grasped him by the collar, panting in harsh gasps. Strange to see ginger nostril hairs by moonlight. He wrenched at Malisse's jacket, trying to right himself against the water. Button thread snapped, exposing the sodden shirt and braces. Instantly, Clem visualized his father seated at the writing desk in the best room, bowed over in shirt sleeves and braces.

Lili was in the doorway, gripping the frame.

"Swim Clem!" She stretched out her free hand.

Malisse gripped and tightened his arm around Clem's neck, pressing against his throat. Clem flailed about, trying to free himself. The man's grip held him until something – a toy train engine – snagged under his foot. For a moment he lost balance. Now Clem held Malisse, motionless, and found himself staring into his father's face.

Clem grasped for Lili's hand. She hauled him towards her until the current caught them. Brown waters foamed about them and turned them over and over. He glimpsed people huddled and squatting under the arches, clothes stuck to their legs, streams of water dripping into the dust. Lili was the current pulling on him; pulling him under.

April

Lou

Lou cocked her head upward towards him as he perched on the roof of the bike shed, legs swinging.

"It's a proper spring day," she said.

She had stowed her bike, thrown her bags down and sprawled on the grass.

"Let's see the drawing," she said.

Clem jumped down. He held out a drawing. The school building was there, technically well-proportioned, the bricks shaded, patches of them drawn in and the rather odd Victorian cupola on the top. And in front, smiling up at the viewing point, her hair tousled from cycling, was Lou: her and yet not her. And, curiously, cross-legged next to her... a small boy holding out a picture.

"You and I understand – imaginary things," she said.

Clem turned and swung his legs down over the roof. Holding on by his arms he lowered himself until he was hanging from the roof beam. He slowly raised his legs to form a right-angle with his body.

She went on, "It's as though we live in two countries at once, but only one where people are allowed to dream with no-one to say, 'But, naturally, a world without prisons is impossible…'"

A blue horse in a purple field. It was the first painting Bob Kay had done. He wouldn't speak – just sat. The Deputy Head had inspected her classroom for signs of slackness on her or the pupil's part. She had probably heard that there was too much drama and art going on since the teacher she shared with at first had moved out to the dining room.

Nora Carp rotated the painting. "What is this, Bob? Have you ever seen a blue horse? No? Because there is no such thing."

Billy looked steadily at the ground. Carp put her finger under his chin and lifted it.

"And we don't paint things that aren't real, do we? Otherwise we might get confused and start telling lies as well." Lou held back. How should she begin? That a blue horse was a sign of life…?

…the milky haze on the horizon grew lighter, the blue showing through as though a schoolchild had smudged it with chalk. Fern sat on the end of the jetty, the collar of her trench coat pulled up around her ears; her image etched against the sky. After a while she retraced her steps along the jetty and crouched beside Lou.

Fern's lips were touching Robin's, "b-b-b-b-b." She tickled his lips with a sound like beating on a drum skin, "dub-a-dub-a-dub."

The blanket was spread out under the ruined brick works wall. A gnarled hawthorn twisted out of the stone step. A little way off was the wharf from where the farm produce used to chug to the early morning markets in London; grain and fresh meat, eggs from the settlement. The Colony of settlers had escaped the filth of London in search of country air and the New Jerusalem. From here some would depart for another continent. Fern stretched her bare arms, lifted Robin above her head and gave him a little shake. He chuckled sleepily.

Lou leaned back and looked up into the boughs of the lanky ash. It was peaceful here. The Colony was still a farm, even though the next stage of emigration had stopped during the wars. Not far off people were picking cabbages and pulling leeks and onions.

Fern said, "I think of those colonists, preparing to take a step into the unknown. How they believed in a new life, how eager they were to grasp their second chance."

"England's shadow," said Lou

"Poverty?"

"If there had been no war my father might have taken us out to Africa to run a colony for the poor."

She picked a dandelion clock and blew – one, two, three, four times and a trail of floss drifted through the air. Robin blinked as some seed settled on his nose. Fern put her hand behind his head and blew.

"Standing on the brink." Lou said. "What do you think I should do Fern?"

"About life? I don't know – sometimes I think it's easier having the decision made for you by a little baggage of bones like this." She patted Robin's back.

"Oh don't say that Fern. I'm sorry… I didn't mean…"

"It doesn't have to be brought up – it's always there. Now let's see. What do you think Lou should do, Robin?"

She lowered Robin towards her face and made little clicking sounds with her tongue against her teeth. Robin bicycled with his legs and arms.

"Look. He says you should follow the one who rides a bicycle."

"But Clem doesn't," laughed Lou.

"Closest thing to the madcap motorcyclist."

"Hardly madcap. But he knows lots of things and he's not full of old hypocritical guff that some 'holier-than-thou' folks come out with."

"He's genuine and good natured and doesn't chase after you with a gun. Has he had a sweetheart before?"

"I expect so, but then he was at the front from the age of eighteen. How could you kiss someone with people dying all around you?"

Fern turned Robin onto his tummy on the blanket. She moved his legs like a swimmer's.

"I'm sure he's going to be able to do some of the things other children do. It's just slower."

Lou jumped up and leaned her back against the portion of the brick works wall that remained. She felt the grain of the stone through her cotton blouse. All over Europe cities had gone back to the state they were in when the City Colony in London was founded.

"Perhaps I could do something more with my life," she said.

"I know," said Fern, patting Robin's back. "I can't help thinking of marriage as an end of freedom. Let's take this one to see the old tractor frames."

Old metal junk still littered the countryside. Like that crashed bomber. Was it still there?

...the boys who combed this stretch for souvenirs, collecting shrapnel and bits of twisted metal, aluminium from planes and scraps of parachute silk. Fern's cousin made junk sculptures out of the bits he collected from the bombed out houses. It wasn't only the humans that were evicted by bombing; Lou had seen rats streaming out of a collapsing cellar. People said they had infested the mortuary. So they put the corpses on the balconies until the carts came to fetch them.

They trudged silently side-by-side, their hands deep in their pockets and their collars up against the wind, making for the library. A page of newspaper flapped ahead of them in the road. The campaign in Germany was being stepped up with attacks on chemical works and airfields. Last night it was Dresden – where the older girls at school used to go for their cultural week before the war. Rose Brown had shown Lou a picture of a church with a dome and, in front of it, a smiling German woman who had spoken to them about her pride in her city.

Clem

The postcard lay on the desk, slightly faded with sunlight. Reuben had sent it from Dresden before the war. Clem laid it next to the plate in *Richardson and Corfiato* showing the *Rathhaus* in Munster with its pyramidal structure. Both had something satisfyingly triangular about them, though the *Frauenkirche* had been circular in the horizontal plane before being powdered into grains of sand.

He felt directionless; not how he had imagined falling in love. Perhaps it was impossible; to love amongst so much loss. Solid structures had disintegrated, crushing lives. Both love and architecture had become equally inconceivable.

There was a day when he had stood in front of the statue of Frederick Augustus of Saxony, streets radiating across a wasteland. Nearby two women clung, silently, to each other. The colour of stone showed under the charred black. The buckled side of a building still cleaved to the vertical like a folly in a desert. That was the moment he found himself giving up architecture. Afterwards the thrill had ebbed from the rare books room with its plans and elevations, leaving a dry heat. He had sat in the *Lit. and Phil. Library* when the bomb on the Quayside made the shelves shudder, shedding dust into the air and clogging his throat. When he returned, it was to read history. There would be no more architecture.

The surface of Reuben's postcard seemed smudged, a trick of the eye perhaps. He lifted it and realised that it was blotted with tears.

The shaving mirror was flecked with pale silver-grey corrosion spots He had let his beard grow for nearly the whole three weeks holiday. He felt along the blade of the razor. He could never quite see the sideburn strip properly in this mirror. Leo had told him that there was a blind spot flying a Spitfire and a danger that the enemy might come close and ambush from behind. Clem had grown adept at staying in people's blind spot. But Lou was different.

She would be here shortly. He had seen her a couple of times over Easter; to walk in the Colony and to hear Nat Gonella and his band playing at the Palladium. They had even danced, the warmth of her body making him feel it might be possible to tell her things. But what exactly? A boundary had been crossed long ago when his mother and father, cousins, were forced to marry. He should tell her before things got too serious, before there was another transgression.

Clem splashed his face with icy cold water and rubbed it with a rough towel.

Upstairs Lou explored his bookshelves. "So this is your hiding place. Your armoury of books in their dust jackets.' She squinted sideways at the spine of a large buff-coloured cover with brown print, *The Art of Architecture*."

"I'm sorry about Ida. I hadn't realized she knew something about your father," said Clem

"I was going to tell you today anyway. I didn't know how you'd feel about it… only I wouldn't like you to hear about it from anyone else."

She walked a couple of paces and stood by the window. Wisps of hair had escaped from the roll and lay against her neck

"You're a historian, Clem."

He felt an ache.

"You don't have to tell me Lou," he said.

"Oh but I do," she replied.

She turned to face him. Her face was in shadow, a frame of light round her head as she stood in the window.

"My father went to prison for a year. It was for a crime I believe he did not commit. He was a top officer in the Mission."

"Oh Lou." He took her hand. She shook him away.

"He was breaking down under the strain of the war. A moment's distraction and he walked out of a shop without paying for a book." Her eyes filled with tears.

She let him put his arm round her shoulder and kiss her cheek and her eyes where the tears were falling. This was the moment to tell her... He moved closer to her and she didn't move away.

Raven

Raven flew with the fighters above the river. Would there be an end for her if she was shot out of the sky like one of these flying machines? She was as old and new as clouds. She surveyed the battlefield after the fighting had passed on. The back wall and buttresses of a barn stood nearby, a stone roof hanging like washing dangling on a propped line. She listened to memories that people had hidden away for safe keeping. There were things she had seen that puzzled her. After removing his uniform an SS officer sunbathed in his yard at home; unbuttoning his collar, he turned his face toward the sun. A child ran and jumped onto his knee, burying her head in the smell of wool, coal tar and tobacco. The following day Raven watched the same man order children and their parents to be herded into trains.

A hot, salt gush of putrefying flesh assaulted her. She moved towards the barn and a sulphurous stench half-triggered the scavenging animal in her. Human bodies were stacked as though someone had tidied them up, intending to return later to remove them. From somewhere near the top came a moan and a slight movement. Her stomach turned as she shoved a leg aside to free the man. She hauled him to the stalls where cattle used to stand, now open to the sky. Opening his shirt at the collar she saw the *Erkennungsmarke,* an oval tin disc stamped with his unit, soldier number and blood type; the lower half would be broken along the perforation when he was pronounced dead. She dribbled water into his mouth from his bottle, but the effort to move had been his last.

Carefully, Raven detached the chain and *Erkennungsmarke* from the dead soldier's neck and fastened it round her own. She squashed the feathers of her raven cloak underneath his uniform, tucking in the edges. In the inner pocket the documents were intact; a *Soldbuch*, which read 'Wolfgang Peters' and a photo of him in military dress. His rank had been *Hauptmann* and an official had listed his equipment in a fine looping script. She would need this if she were stopped at a roadblock by the military police.

The *Kommando* was based in a low, windowless brick building with a corrugated iron roof. Three moths, brown and cream tapestry wings open, were sunning themselves against the bricks. Crickets shrilled from where they crouched in little gaps in the mortar. A *Kübelwagen* and a motorbike were parked outside. As Raven entered the office the *Bezirksleiter* looked up.

The *Hauptman* extended his gloved hand and Vogelweide returned the salute, *"Heil Hitler,"*

Raven handed him an official envelope. "Just a routine move. They want you in Dresden on official business. Refugees need to be registered and identities assigned."

Vogelweide studied the letter, giving Raven a chance. As the door slammed, she penetrated the man's thoughts and saw that he was hiding, even from himself. He clicked his tongue and tutted. So he was to be moved again, just when he was in control of this district.

It wasn't long before the knock he had been expecting sounded at the door. "I've brought the Quaker, Clemens, to you," said the clerk.

"All right," Vogelweide leaned back in his chair. "Bring him in."

This was a man suspected of assisting Jews to escape with fake papers; one of these so called "idealists".

So this was the German pacifist, thought Raven. She was curious about how interrogation worked but the *Bezirksleiter* whose form she occupied was a disappointing inquisitor; too ill at ease with himself under Clemens' gaze; too aware of his secret Jewish blood fighting with his German blood - like oil and water, they would not mix.

Vogelweide thought of Himmler's speech on eliminating the bacterium that infected even those who did their duty without flinching. Clemens continued to stare at him.

Vogelweide must take control, but instead of reading out the allegations against Clemens, he found himself slipping his hand inside his shirt and drawing out the locket with the picture of his mother inside. He flipped the catch with his thumb; the yellow tinge of his mother's hair was not as he remembered it. His unease deepened.

Raven sifted through Vogelweide's memories. The room filled with the scent of apples and Raven found herself in an orchard. A boy of about seven or eight cried inconsolably pulling at his mother's skirt, "My apple tree mamma."

His mother continued furiously hacking at a branch of the tree.

"This is as it must be my little man." Hack-hack. "For our beautiful country to survive we must cut out the dead wood." Hack-hack.

She was a powerful woman, the bare, freckled, muscular arms toasted to a golden brown.

"Let me help you mother."

She laughed at him as the tears flushed his face and salted his mouth, "Not yet my little man, my Auguste. You will be tall and strong enough one day."

Vogelweide tapped the photograph with his hand. "My mother," he said. "She died when I was a boy. They tried surgery to cut out the cancer. He was a Jew, the doctor." He

171

flushed. The interrogation had got off on the wrong foot. "Later I came to realize the Jews are the disease," he added hastily. He peered at Clemens. "What of the question of mixed blood? What about *Rassenverrat*, betrayal of the race?" He felt his mouth contort involuntarily.

Clemens cleared his throat. "You loved your mother. I, too. And my sisters and brothers"

"Beware, Quaker. I have a document here that would seal your fate. My signature could have you removed to a forced labour camp." Vogelweide was sweating. He put his head in his hands.

"Are you quite well?" Clemens asked.

"Yes of course." He tried to regain his composure. "Clemens, you have…" He squinted at the charge sheet, "evidently been falsifying documents to assist the avoidance of punishment by those contravening the race laws. An offence punishable in law by hard labour."

After he had signed the document consigning Clemens to the next transport to *Buchenwald*, he listened for a moment to the choke and chunter of the *kübelwagons* coming and going on the road. He freshened up in the washroom at the back of his office, in preparation for his journey to Dresden. There would be no time to bath at home.

172

Slave labourers forced to emigrate by the Nazis were mixing with those expelled by the Soviets. They poured into Dresden from Lithuania, Ukraine, White Russia, Georgia and Azerbaijan; Poles, Czechs and Germans from the East. Surely this city of culture would never be targeted by the Allied bombers.

On an airfield in Britain, Clements sniffed the cold night air and blew on the tips of his fingers poking out of the fingerless gloves Louisa had knitted him. A wind was blowing up from the East. The Squadron's ground staff was lined up by the trolleys with the tractor up front ready to load the *Lancasters'* bomb bays. Navigation and radio equipment had been checked. Clements hauled himself into the pilot's seat.

"Do you ever think of what's happening down below?" Louisa had asked during his last leave,

He hadn't answered at first. "Well, of course, we only bomb military targets. The weapons we have now, they're capable of great precision…"

They were a good crew. He watched Blower glance at the tally of beer mugs on the fuselage. The missions were counted in the success of getting back to the bar.

It was dark when they rumbled over the runway. "Ready?" Clements asked and `Cricket' juddered slightly before the lift into the night sky. Ahead was the stream of planes, with more joining from other airfields. There was cloud below, starched by a brittle moonlight. Leonard pored over his maps.

The train from *Buchenwald* to Dresden was packed even though it was some time after midnight. Vogelweide felt vindicated – he had been sent to look at the refugee problem, to assist in organizing registration in Dresden and to disperse as many as possible so they would not tax the resources of a city already over stretched. Hitler had a particular interest in the city with its Zwinger museum, Rococo art and the Japanese Palace which kept a collection of classical sculptures.

They were travelling through the industrial district now with its coal depots, cigarette factories, glass, lead, paint and chemical works; Germany was pulling herself up by the bootstraps. And getting there – a great nation in the era of science. To act as *Bezirksleiter* in Dresden could be seen as promotion Vogelveide told himself, though he couldn't quite throw off the feeling of queasiness; the bad blood working in him. He had coped with the shock when his son, Otto, turned up the genealogy in his school research. He had warned Otto about the vile disease affecting his racial purity and acted quickly to keep the school teachers from discovering the secret, but now he felt he might be losing control.

As they drew into Dresden the train jolted violently and Vogelweide was pressed against the window by a woman who fell against him. The sudden slam reverberated through Raven.

She dragged the body she was occupying out of the compartment and down the corridor.

Vogelweide poked his head out of a window. A troupe of little girls in carnival dress ran wildly between knots of people carrying suitcases and packs. The nausea made his head swim as the girls passed close by. The carnival leader was elongated, the costume towering on some kind of frame inside a dress of old garments stitched together. The top half of the figure swayed above its occupant, its board arms stuck with fabric which flapped as it moved. It was crowned with a skeletal face; the picture of hunger. The figure lurched towards the train, hollowed eyes staring blindly at Vogelweide. He rapped on the window and flapped his hands, but the miscreants only laughed at him.

Outside the station the streets were full of refugees waiting for him to arrive and organise them; twenty-six thousand POWs as well as all of the refugees from the East. And these preposterous carnival grotesques had the audacity to laugh at him.

The air raid siren sounded. An accident? Dresden was safe; the Florence of the North. There was no need to build concrete bunkers here. The siren continued. People leapt out of the train and sprinted for shelter. There was no doubt that these people needed control. The platform was filling up, seething with people scurrying like like rats at the first sign of danger. The train stank of sweat and fear, but it was best to stay put. A few minutes later he heard the beat and grind of

175

bombers. They would empty their load on the outskirts, the industrial area. More bombers followed and then more and more; wave after wave of them.

He glanced at his watch. It was eight minutes past ten. Cracking light shocked the yard into red, blue, green. The throbbing from above was so loud he felt his head would break. If he squinted upwards he could see the sky through the roof windows, glowing like a red ember. People jumped off the train and scattered like ants. A couple loaded down with pots and pans clung to each other. From further down the carriage came an interminable screaming.

The target was blasted with colour by the pathfinder marker flares and the plane interior lit up as though an electric bulb had been switched on. There was no flak. Bombs dropped below in linear formation.

The radio crackled, "Bomb doors ready."

"Drop," came the shout.

"She's away," said Blower and then, "Incendiaries away."

The sky was illuminated with an undersea pallor, an artificial moonlight cast by the burning below.

There was a long low moan and then Leonard's voice shouting a list of places. "Lubeck, Cologne, Berlin, Hamburg,"

It was what they had all suspected, but had not admitted. What had Clements told Louisa about the weapons being capable of great precision? So precise that now he could

176

describe the snow over Hamburg; the planes flying so low that they were able to see the flakes caking the corners of the streets and roofs. And if they had refused to obey orders?

The fires down below were already blazing out of control. Smoke swirled out of a smouldering wasps' nest of cloud. Behind them the sky was a dirty rose smudged the colour of the flames. The heat in the cockpit intensified.

"Essen, Aachen, Arnhem," intoned Leonard.

They gained height as instructed and switched on the oxygen.

A flurry of sparks flew in at the window of the train and stung Vogelweide's cheek. There was a smell of singeing. He slammed the window across feeling the warmth of the metal. It was getting hotter in the packed corridor. Vogelweide brushed his arm over his forehead.

Raven began to struggle inside his body. Two silent children stared up at him. They were not tall enough to see what was going on outside the window. He pulled off his jacket and shirt and his skin began to stretch as though clawed from the inside. His eyes glazed over and his stomach rippled before a wedge appeared at his chest and the texture of his skin changed, waves of black feather fronds spiking it. When his mouth opened he emitted an unearthly squawk.

Vogelweide tried to control the waves of nausea. Was this a fever of some kind? Free of his top clothes he felt better. Smoke was filtering into the carriage. The train jerked and he was thrown against another passenger, a woman who stank of vodka. He wrenched himself away from her clasp. An hour had passed since the train first drew into the station. Outside, dazed people lathered with dirt were pushing to get onto the train.

"My God. My God. We are burning in hell." cried a woman.

Guards tried to move people back. The heat was suffocating. He opened the door, descended and elbowed his way through the crowds streaming into the station.

"Don't go outside," warned a man carrying one child, another hanging onto his coat. "It's a volcano. There's lava running in the streets, no air and a terrible wind."

Outside the station the sky was pitted with brilliant diamonds. The stink must be chemicals going up. He ran with the crowd, hardly noticing that he was treading on hot charcoals. He must keep his feet out of the melting tar that had been a road. On the crowded *Grosse Garten* a voice cried, "Repent, repent ye sinners, before it is too late."

There was a rumble of planes. A second wave? He must get underground. The cellars would be ovens; where the fire raged the occupants would bake. Yet what choice was there? Vogelweide leaned down and put his face to a grating that let air into a basement.

"I am an officer, sent here to organise the refugee problem. I can pay." He waved a sheaf of notes in a man's face.

The seizures were coming faster. His body convulsed and he fell to the ground, his mouth wide open. The beak came first and a few wet feathers. Raven's head was freed, but his gorge and gullet gripped her. She heaved. His skin stretched and thinned, then tore. Someone reached in hands slippery with sweat, gripped the feathers and pulled.

Someone began a hymn and more voices joined in. It spread like wildfire. Planes moaned above. The farmer pulled at the feathers, which parted for a moment revealing a woman's soft breast. Raven shook herself free. She laid for a moment, exhausted, a bundle of feathers. Then she gathered herself and slipped outside.

Behind her Vogelweide sat up, his shoulders heaving. "I am *Mischling*. I have two Jewish grandparents."

"What of it?" came a rough rural voice. "This is our grave. The bombs will not recognise Aryans, Nordics or Slavs."

Raven perched on the *Stallhof* as the cloister crumbled. She watched the fire. Fire was as old as Raven, as old as the first night. The fire caught Raven's tail feathers as she swung upwards. Smoke filled her lungs. Sparks bit her throat. The city was melting like candles.

She urged her wings into flight, before her feathers became too brittle, powdering into dust. She soared above a city that looked like thousands of glowing eyes burning through the sockets of buildings; a cloth full of holes. As flames shot around her it seemed that she was on the far side of the cloth of the sky, from where stars twinkled through the rips.

As she flew higher the city was a beacon of purple and white. Furious sparks rose on the thermal winds. And still the incendiaries fell. Raven flew higher; fifty, a hundred, a hundred and fifty miles. Still she saw a glow. She turned, circling downwards, back towards the beacon of the city, keeping pace with a lone bomber.

The men were silent inside the plane. They looked down on one spire toppled from the *Sophienkirche* and on the *Frauenkirche* naked without her dome

Raven crawled into the heart of the fire. How would she restore the sun to the sky? The buildings wept melting glass. When the last bomb fell Raven closed her eyes and laid down on the molten glass as around her the world collapsed.

As dawn broke, fires continued to rage along the *Prager, Augustus, Moritz* and *Ring Strassen*. A dismembered leg swung from a charred tree. Two figures stood on the outer edge of the ring of fires staring at Raven's body; a heap of feathers, blood, human and bird bones crushed together. Feathers were mangled; the sternum was cracked in two like the keel of a boat and the vertebral column had collapsed like a row of dominoes. All that was left were two eyes. Blood seeped into a gutter.

Clem examined Raven. He heaved the carcass onto his back, holding the head tenderly. She would be buoyed by the waters of the Elbe until she was carried out to sea and her bones washed clean of blood and feather.

The bombing had caused ruptures in the sewage pipe system and a flow of faeces was emptying into the river. Raven sank into the fluid soup and lay suspended there before drifting for miles, half-conscious in the warmth of the foetid flow. Next year the banks of the river would bloom with lilies.

Summer Term, 1950

The Man who wanted to live forever

May

Lou

Lou let the book lie in her lap a moment. Her eyes rested on Robin's face as he watched sunlight flicker across the wall. There was a movement of tree shadow and the lace nets billowed. Robin had moods like the weather, but today he was still. Fern was sleeping, tired by the night feeds. Lou dusted her father's books while Robin lay propped on cushions. Though her father's heart was failing, this was something she could still do for him. She lingered over Gerard Manly Hopkins' *Collected Poetry*, remembering how she loved to hear him reading passages aloud; how carefully each book was packed whenever her parents moved as young officers.

Robin made a lolling sound with his tongue and Lou called back to him. Clem had reacted sympathetically to her revelation about her father. A young man who had been brought up in a good Methodist family with Quaker connections might have thought twice about courting someone whose father had been in prison for a year, but he saw it as she did.

She leaned over and tickled Robin's feet. He kicked flatly and chuckled. Fern massaged his legs and arms each day so that his muscles would firm, tighten and fold. The year was flying by. At school Daphne still slammed her desk lid at odd times but Lou understood more now. She knew the younger child had heard the shot that killed her mother, pregnant by a Canadian soldier, the night her father came back; how Bob Kay was evacuated to Wales and returned to find both his parents dead; how June's father went missing in action and her mother went to hospital and died of brain sickness. At the end of each afternoon they would sit in a circle and tell their stories. They were the Barnado's class; the ones no-one else wanted to teach, but Lou knew what it was to be propelled off course by war, or distracted as her father had been that day.

Robin made little suck-blow noises. She leaned over, gathered him in her arms, held him to her shoulder and rocked him.

"What do you think, Robin, what do you think of it all?"

Lou hung back and let Fern walk ahead. She didn't want to intrude. Fern stopped walking and stood looking out to sea.

The letter telling about her Uncle Lance had come that morning – another who had 'died fighting for his country'.

After a few minutes Lou went and stood next to Fern. The dark form of a ship stretched along the horizon.

"Years ago," said Fern, "Uncle Lance would tease my mother about going overboard on the cooking front, 'No need to kill the fatted calf – I was only here last week, Vera.' He didn't really approve of us becoming Seventh Day Adventists. He'd say to me, 'Don't lose your sense of fun, kid.'"

They automatically kept an eye out for signs of invasion, even though the enemy was supposed to be weakened.

After a few minutes Fern continued, "We'll never see Uncle Lance again – but it's all right, because he died for his country. That makes it brave and good."

She looked back at their line of footprints in wet mud, the further away ones already filling up; the closer ones crumbling at the edges. Lou's footsteps were straighter.

"I want to know whether he died all in one piece, Lou, or torn up into little scraps. Do you think that's unhealthy?"

Lou took Fern's hand and squeezed it. Fern squeezed back.

"We're not supposed to think that way, are we?"

The coastguard's hut was not far off. He might turn them back with a warning. They jumped the winding salty inflows from the sea. Garish twists of aluminium thrust up, cracking the crust of mud, gleaming like a cache of warrior shields, polished for burial with their owner.

"Oh look," exclaimed Lou, "this is where that *Lancaster* went down two years ago. My father told me about it. The fuselage has almost disappeared, or been pinched, but little bits and pieces keep poking up from the marsh when it dries out."

"The strange thing is, Lou, that the grown-ups try to keep it from us, as if we don't know."

Lou made a circular frame with her fingers, screwing up her eye to peer at the ship on the horizon. Her mother had taken her to visit her father in Wormwood Scrubs last night. It shook her; as though she had crossed a bridge to another side. Someone further down the corridor was banging a bucket like a gong. Father hadn't been himself. The conversation was short; she must work hard at school; he needed her to do that. He was continuing his ministry in prison; counselling other prisoners.

The ship seemed to be getting closer.

"They don't tell you the real things, like what food tastes like when you've got to force it down you before you go into a hole in the ground to wait your turn to play at dead men," said Fern.

Without warning she set off running. Lou followed. They ran and ran along the edge sometimes sloshing in their lace ups through the fringes of a wave. Further out were dark shipping lanes on the horizon where men and boys polished their guns and dreamed of home. At last Lou doubled up, breath sharp and prickling, a stitch in her side.

"I'll tell you the story of the boy who wanted to live forever," she called.

"Now who would want to do that?" panted Fern as she slowed a little ahead of Lou.

"Perhaps it's Italian or perhaps it's Bavarian or French or Russian – I don't know. I got it from my grandmother at Millfield, the one who helps the fallen girls. She got it from Betty Threadgold at the POW camp."

"There was once a boy who lived with his family in a little village of stone houses. In the centre of the village was a bridge across a stream. The stream swelled in winter and ran to a trickle in summer. They lived on the edge of a war zone and every few weeks or months the fighting would come close and another few of the village people would go away to die. The boy's brother went away to war and did not return. The boy asked his mother and father where he could find the place where he could live forever. They told him there was no such place, but he knew they were keeping the truth from him. If there were no war then surely his mother and father would live for ever. So he set off to find the place.

He hadn't gone far before he met an old man with a beard tickling his chest, wheeling a barrow of stones down the side of a mountain.

'Do you know of the place where I can live forever?' asked the boy.

The old man answered him, 'That I don't know but I can tell you that my task is to bring every rock and stone down from that mountain top to make a flat plain. Only when I have finished will my time come.'

'How long will that take you?' asked the boy.

'Now that's a hard one; maybe a hundred years.'

'Thank you, but that's not enough for me.'

The boy trudged on under a scorching sun, his mouth parched, until he entered the shade of a great forest where the trees were as endless as marching soldiers. Somewhere in the forest was the sound of a small axe: pock-pock pock-pock. The boy followed the sound until he came to a clearing full of the stumps of trees, a pile of dead branches in the centre. Among the trees at the edge an old man with a beard tickling his belly was chopping a branch with a small axe.

'Do you know of the place where I can live forever?' asked the boy.

The old man answered, 'That I don't know, but I can tell you that my task is to chop down every tree in this forest. Only when I have finished will my time come.'

'How long will that take you?' asked the boy.

'The old man stroked his beard, "Maybe two hundred years.'

'Thank you, but that's not enough for me.'

The boy journeyed on, footsore and weary, for many days and nights until he stood on the lip of a ring of hills, a vast lake spread before him. As the boy approached the edge of the lake he saw an old man with a beard tickling his knees sitting on the shore of stones. He lifted a little cup at his lips. Every so often he dipped the cup in the water, then raised it to his lips again.

'Do you know of the place where I can live forever?' asked the boy.

The old man answered, 'That I don't know but I can tell you that my task is to drink every last drop of this lake. Only when I have finished will my time come.'

'How long will that take you?' asked the boy.

The old man nodded, 'Maybe three hundred years.'

'Thank you, but that won't do for me.'

The boy kept on walking. It grew cold and the frost spangled his breath and bit his knuckles. He shivered and wrapped his arms around himself. At last he came to a castle of ice on a glass mountain. The boy climbed the steep track that was hacked into the ice and arrived at the door of the castle where he knocked. An old man with a white beard trailing along the ground opened the door.

'Come in,' he said. 'You're just in time.'

The old man and the boy lived there for a long time exchanging stories every evening. But one morning the boy opened his window in the tower and a fresh breeze blew in. Thoughts of his mother and father and his little village far away woke in the boy's heart.

He went to the old man and said, 'I long to see my mother's face again. I would like to visit my home one time more.'

The old man said, 'But here is what you were seeking.'

The boy replied, 'I have lost everything for this.'

The old man gave him a steed from his stable that could gallop faster than the wind. Before he left the old man warned him, 'Be sure not to let your feet touch the ground.'

The steed galloped past a vast dry hollow. On a lip of stones lay a pile of bones and scattered fragments of china. The steed galloped past a great plain of dry stumps of trees where the wind groaned. They sped past a flat plain littered with rocks. Then the boy saw ahead of him a city whose buildings stretched as far as the eye could see, far across the valley. After a time he came to a familiar little bridge with a stream running beneath it. But the stone houses had vanished and, instead, huge towers reared up *before him with hundreds of blank eyes. None of the people knew him and he recognised no-one.*

The boy turned his steed round and headed back to the glass mountain, past the flat plain of stones, past the waste of dry tree stumps, past the pile of bones and fragments of china. When he reached the road leading up to the ice castle he beheld an old man. His cart was piled with shoes and its wheel had stuck in a rut of packed snow.

'Please spare a little of your time to help me,' begged the old man. The boy remembered that he must not let his feet touch the ground.

'I cannot,' said the boy.

'Surely you who have all the time in the world could spare a few moments to help one whose time will soon be spent.'

He speaks the truth, thought the boy, I must help him. He slipped from the horse's back. The instant his feet touched the earth the old man sprang up like a young sapling and grasped the boy by the wrist.

'At last I have you. I've worn out all the shoes in my cart pursuing you. I am death and your time has come.'

With that, the boy crumbled to dust."

Fern was silent. The ship had moved across the horizon towards the land. Lou picked up a spiral ridged piece of aluminium frame like the skeleton of some strange otherworldly sea creature. The scatter of aircraft parts looked casually expectant, as though a child had dismantled a clock and simply needed the clue to start putting it back together again.

*

The house was in darkness. Lou heard a stifled sort of sob as she crept towards the bathroom. She felt her way along the dado rail rather than put the light on and disturb her father. The bathroom door was ajar. Inside, Fern was curled up on the floor, arms hugging knees and hands clenched. Her face was pressed into the rag rug. Lou crouched down on the floor beside her.

"Fern?" whispered Lou, putting her arm on Fern's. "What's the matter my sweet one." She stroked her arm and after a minute or so Fern unfurled a little and Lou helped her into a sitting position. She put her arm round her shoulders and Fern leaned against her, her face wet.

"I don't know if I can do it Lou…" she said

"You mean…"

"All of it. The nightmares. The night feeds. The forever of it.

"Oh Fern." Lou hugged her friend and smoothed Fern's hair, which hung in midnight black ropes, crimped from plaiting.

"When it happened… the… the rape… when he was pressing down on me I went into a tight small space. I concentrated hard on keeping breathing. But I wasn't really *there*."

Lou rocked Fern gently.

"I've thought about it a lot. Do you think that to them you seem submissive? You go limp and they interpret it as compliance, she-wolves submitting to the leader of the pack?"

"You have to preserve yourself before all else, in whatever way you can," said Lou.

"If you went to a death camp perhaps you would go right down inside yourself, become very small."

"They weakened the Jews first didn't they – made them..."

"Like women – they thought it would take their manhood or womanhood – away so that they could take control."

"You mustn't think of all of this," said Lou.

"If I had resisted it would have meant taking the gun and killing him while he was on top of me. It was lying on the floor not far away."

"But you didn't."

"I thought he was sick... needed treatment..." She slumped her head back against the bath and then forward into her hands. "It's like... do you remember how we felt on *VE* day? Victory and peace but the victory and peace felt no different from the war."

Of course she remembered... and the weeks afterwards too...

...it had been raining for days with no break until now and, chances were, it would rain again before long, a relentless emptying of the sky. The shelter was watertight, built of drifted timbers, a khaki waxed-cotton awning stretched across; a knife slit to fit it over the timber uprights and bound on with rope. It was constructed on the outer edge of the rocks with the sheer face at the back, a view of the bay framed by triangular struts and canvas flaps. They thought it must be a soldier on leave who had put it there.

Lou knew she should be feeling joyful. Victory. Rain splashed into a channel that was also being filled up by the tide below their rock. A honking, mourning sound welled out of the sky and Lou leaned forward to watch the skein of geese arc across the frame, forming a trailing V. V for victory; V for V1s and the long 10 seconds and for V2s. She dreamt about running from bombs that pursued her across fields.

They had been living for this time for ever and now it had come. Fern and she had dressed up to walk though the streets and watch the parties on *VE* day. But there was so much mending to do. And when her father was released no-one said sorry and it didn't mean he could go back to the Mission.

The geese flew. Long necks stretched out, wings beating in time with each other, honking in flight.

Clem

Frank had wanted to be propped up against the bolster and some feather pillows. Frieda had set out the phrenological head with the map of the human qualities marked out across the cranium.

"Well, Copperknob," he said, running his hand through Clem's hair. He paused, then stroked round in a circle. "You've got quite an imagination. Don't live in your dreams to the detriment of reality though. You won't make much money, but you could be happy."

He applied the fingertips of both hands to Clem's head and pressed as he moved them from the centre down to the ears on each side.

"My advice is – don't keep your sadness to yourself. Lou will have told you what happened to me – to us – a few years ago. You see she believes in having everything out in the open.

I do, too, Copperknob." He pressed an area to the right of Clem's skull. "You're not an ambitious man are you?"

Clem shifted further down in the chair and tipped it back slightly on its legs as Frank held his chin and felt the back of his head.

"I'm not sure."

"If you hide things, a volcano can build up underneath. It can tip you over the edge, so you do things without even knowing you are doing them, like walking out of a shop with a book." He looked piercingly at Clem. "Louisa told me you'd had a period of neurasthenia."

"I found my experiences during the war – and after – difficult to face up to…"

"And you still feel that way?"

"Yes."

"All I ask is that you speak about it. An illness of the mind can happen to any of us. A simple absent-minded action can – I won't say ruin – but alter your life irrevocably. Nothing is the same afterwards. Turn your chair to face me. That's it. Louisa's mother, my wife Frieda, and my daughter, they stood by me. Frieda helps people who are unjustly accused; ostracised by society through no fault of their own. Like Fern."

He gauged the shape of Clem's frontal lobes.

"Room for intelligence. Make sure you use it," he said, smiling.

Clem mumbled assent. Here was another moment when he could have spoken out, presenting itself without warning. Yet still he could not bring himself to say that his father and mother were cousins, forced to marry to save the family name.

"It is easier to swim with the tide, isn't it? We don't want to risk being tarred with the same brush. Are we to blame if we keep silence? I expect you had Jewish friends at university?"

Frank gave him a pat as though to indicate that the reading was over. Clem moved the chair back to the side of the room and replaced the white pottery head on the side table under the window.

"Don't think I want to pry," said Frank.

"No of course not," Clem replied. "Yes I had a Jewish friend, Reuben. Read chemistry. Killed in '44. Normandy. Gold beach."

"I'm sorry," said Frank.

"Aren't you bitter about what happened to you?" asked Clem.

"No, not bitter. I've prayed often for the Mission itself – but there was nothing to forgive and nothing to be bitter about."

Raven

Clem had been drifting down the Elbe for days. North of Dresden and a little downstream he had found the boat washed against a fallen tree. Drains and pipes had been shattered and people drank infected water. Islands of turf, scorched and ripped out by the explosions three months ago, still sloshed about the banks and made navigation difficult. On the left hand bank was the hulk of a shattered corn exchange, like the carcass of some great whale beached and rotting.

His meal was makeshift; vegetables from a field at the side of the river cooked on a small fire of broken window frames; bread dipped in the thin soup of potato and beetroot. He gazed at the upward pointing fingers of the broken bridge. A heavy metallic clang sounded from the direction of the docks. He rowed mechanically. From time to time the wind skittered mischievously through the ruins of the city, whirling dust. A cloud of glinting specs of mica and quartz crushed from granite rolled over him, blotting out the water-meadows. He slung his oars into the rowlocks and let the boat drift. It seemed as though it was not only vision but his other senses that were blocked; eyes and ears clogged with dust, even his mouth; only his hands remained.

When the fog cleared he found himself below a bridge between the city and the mountains. Displaced people, their heads bowed, crossed the bridge carrying their possessions on their backs.

He called out, "Tell me; is there a place where we can live forever?"

A woman knelt as he sculled toward the bank. She smiled and uncovered her bundle. Dust glittered in a pool of sun.

"Only when we have worn out our shoes carrying dust from our city will our time come."

Clem nodded to her and poled the boat back into midstream with the longer oar. Usually the bridge was guarded and he would need papers to cross. There were so many people flowing out of the city that progress was slow.

The water was full and high, carrying silt and mud from higher up. Dark slicks like oil, rich with effluent, filmed the surface, scummy along the bank where it clung. Languidly bobbing in the foam was a seal. Or was it a human body, bloated with gas? An arm rose fleetingly to the surface. After a time he realised that another small boat was bumping among the debris. A figure – a woman – leaned over the side and hauled up a corpse, knocking its limp arm into the stern of the boat. She tidied it up, removing bits of stick and weed tangled in the hair.

Clem called softly, so as not to startle her. "Do you know of a place where we can live forever?" he asked, drawing alongside the boat so that their hulls bumped together.

"Now that I don't know," said the woman. She was plump and dressed in a khaki canvas coat. "But only when the whole forest is cut down will my work be done," she said, spreading a cloth and covering the body.

Clem noticed a pile of books in the flat bottom of the barge.

"Yes," she said, as if reading his thought, "We seek out their apartments and collect their books and send them on after them."

When she opened her mouth, Clem saw that she had no teeth and her lips curled under her gums. She pushed the boats apart and he paddled away.

The Elbe slid, sometimes lazily, spreading out across a valley floor, sometimes swiftly through rocky channels choked with human waste. He had slept fitfully against a vertical rough stone on the bank. An old gatepost perhaps or a gravestone. The cemetery was surrounded by a stone wall. He had been rowing the boat for many days and had eaten little. His head felt light. A thrush began singing and he could hear sounds like artillery fire not far away. One wall of the church had been demolished but there was laughter and clattering from further within. There was an astringent smell of yew, invigorating after the rain, and the shouts of children nearby.

Clem struggled to rise and realised he was very weak. He no longer felt hunger. Two mop-haired boys ran into view carrying a rough sack between them, cuffing each other. They began wrestling, a bare-fisted fight with bared teeth and blood drawn. They rolled onto the sack which came loose and bloated, red bellied fungi spilled around them. Among the fungi Clem made out a foot and a hand with rings. There was a hoarse cry from inside the church and the boys scrambled up and started scooping up mushrooms and bloody body parts, piling them back into the bag.

They jumped up and ran, one of them lunging into Clem,

"Tell me; where is the place where we can live forever?" he panted, winded.

One boy grinned, "What are you asking? They are opening the mass graves. We take back what was stolen. We go by night. Only when we have stolen back all that was taken away will our task be ended."

The boy fished in the pocket of his torn jacket and drew out a pair of spectacles in round metal frames. Then, hearing a shout from the church, he scarpered.

Higher voices echoed. Two girls were digging at a patch of vegetation that grew on a grave mound. Rough fingers grubbed up pignut roots and brushed off the soil. They chanted the names of flowers, "Wallflower, day lily, poppy."

Funeral flowers. "White lace, Dead Man's Baccy, poison globes; Lords and Ladies."

Clem came back to consciousness to find himself covered with a white cloth, smooth and richly embroidered. A fire crackled near him and above was a screen carved with animals. The nave was full of smoke. The figures around him were obscured by the smouldering yew. A woman was bending over an iron pot suspended from a frame over a fire below the bare altar. The smell from the pot nauseated and drew him. He thought of the sack of limbs and fungi he had seen earlier. He began sweating and someone bathed his head.

When he came round again, he heard a grunt and felt something nosing his underarm. A large pig was rooting insistently. A man's voice snarled and a cracked hand reached down and slapped the pig's backside, sending it trotting off to one corner. A woman handed him a bowl of soup. She began speaking in halting English.

"Our home was on the battle front. We got caught in between. We lost everything, but we are surviving. We used to have two cows, but now only this pig."

"The Americans and the English have a reconstruction programme," said the man with the harsh voice, "but not for us, not for the poor; only for those who have something worth reconstructing."

One of the others laughed and spat. "We lost everything in twenty four hours."

The woman who had handed him the soup shuffled uncomfortably. "It is safer to live among the dead than among the living. The dead are beyond our reach, and we beyond theirs."

After some time he came to a place that was not marked on any map. The water tanker drove through the gates of *Sandbostel* Concentration Camp and he saw the faces of the people inside looking up. Grey figures stood impassive, hands hanging by their sides. It was hard to tell how old they were and in the grey camp uniform, standing so still, they seemed to be covered in dust. Clem jumped down from the wagon. The man looking at him opened his shirt. The architecture of his ribcage was curved, like a frame slung over with slack nets hung out to dry. He had heard of a church somewhere made of the skeleton of a whale. Clem looked into the man's eyes as though across an immense distance and felt the weight of his own guilt.

As he gazed at the man he found himself in a railway cattle truck, rocking from side to side. He felt the press of people. A couple with a baby next to him were trying to persuade it to swallow some bread dipped in water from the communal tank in the middle of the truck. He felt a gush of air striking through the slats, filtering the sweat of the herded people.

Framed between slats, a boy had broken from another carriage and rolled down an embankment. They watched him running for the woods, willing him to make it before the shot. The boy folded onto the ground.

Someone was humming a tune and someone else picked it up. *Klesma.* A Jewish folk tune. The man who stood before him could be the Professor of Music from the Conservatory or he may have been a street cleaner. From inside his open shirt, the man pulled out a small box and slid the lid open. Clem saw parts of flies and spiders; segmented legs that had broken, dry and disintegrating; a thorax and an abdomen; a wing. Inscribed on the inside of the box were words.

Chaim Gontaz surveyed his museum of arachnids. Each piece could easily be slipped into place above its label. He could do it in a moment. And yet when he held the box up for the Englishman to see, he seemed to be looking at something else and his face was wet.

June

Lou

The swing rose and fell with the movement of the Elm. Their branches would hold after a storm, then fall days later on a windless day. She hoped it was doing Clem good to be staying with her Quaker friends after his neurasthenia had recurred. Yet he seemed subdued with Grace and David.

"Slow down! Slower!" she laughed, out of breath.

He let the swing wind down until it came to rest while he perched on a fallen branch looking toward the Solway.

"You would tell me if you felt... bad, wouldn't you Clem?"

"Of course," he said.

...they leaned their backs against a squat concrete gun emplacement in the old sea wall. A book about Japan was propped between them. With each creep of the tide the sea in the harbour bubbled closer and then retreated.

Lou's new corset dug into her under the arms. "How can you stand these things?" she grumbled. "At least a liberty bodice doesn't dig in and squeeze."

She studied a picture of a lashing female water serpent in glossy green-brown print. Fern's father had obviously never read the book so they sliced the uncut pages with a knife themselves. Another illustration showed fishing boats lying on their side in the harbour and one or two yachts with masts. Their ropes would be clattering against the masts and pennants flapping like the ones at Canvey Island.

They had read about the light in the paper, how terrible it was, like a second sun in the sky lighting up the copper roof of the temple. After the flash and the second sun, a cloud grew. It sent out spores that undid atoms, fingers working deftly inside people, leaving only a shadow to mark where it done its work.

Fern opened the piece of newspaper she had cut out and read aloud; "I saw the skin hanging off my neighbour's legs and arms, like flaps of material. I had my needle and thread in my hands and so began to try and stitch his skin together. I thought I could make it so that it would hold until he got to the hospital. He looked at me, dazed, and I realised that my own skin was peeling away like a snake's when it sloughs it off. The sun came out and it was then that the pain began. Unless I tell my story, each moment will be that moment. People may forget. But the story will live."

Clem

Clem brought a jug of fresh lemon barley water and set it down on the bedside table. Frank's eyes followed him. He indicated Lou's box on the bedside table. Clem lifted the box from the table and traced the webbed-leaf with his finger. Each box was skilfully carved with shapes of nasturtium or ladies mantle and each contained a smaller box with more delicate and intricate carving. He laid them on the gold candlewick bedspread, until in the final one he found a scrap of folded paper, a news paper cutting about Hiroshima.

He looked at Frank and took out his brown leather journal.

"I thought you might like to see this. I could read you a little," he said. Frank nodded.

Clem paused. Frank lifted his hand, moving it painfully to lie on Clem's wrist. He nodded slightly. Clem inserted the key and turned it, as Eva had done before when she read the journal to Lili and him. The script was fine and written in brown ink. He opened the book to show Frank where it was cut out in the centre to leave a box shaped hole. In this hole was another book, also bound in brown leather.

"The larger is the journal of a Nazi prison guard. The other is a female prisoner's. They were written in Auschwitz in 1944.

"They have taken Etty. Is it possible to be a pacifist in that place? It is a death factory. I know this from my father. There are boys there of sound mind; educated. They cannot live with the truth so they pretend it is not happening."

"Shall I go on?"

"I have been working at Auschwitz for three months now. I am both resister and colluder. I cannot tell where the boundary lies or if there is one. Civilisation is a gloss, the sanitized appearance of consensus, maintained by good administration. I am good-mannered, have good taste, am not regarded as crude or vulgar. Indulging in the vulgarity of protest is worse than the threat of death, for then we risk becoming victims. Civilization makes us turn our face away from what we do not wish to see."

Frank nodded, slowly moved his hand towards Clem's and squeezed weakly.

Raven

The evening horizon of dusty lemon clouds was blurred by day-lily orange smoke. The Elbe's fingers tangled with twisted metal, the buckled cross-lacings of a bridge. For a time he rowed and then drifted, feeling tired and old, though not as old as the man who had held out a matchbox of spiders, his flesh parched from within. Chaim Gontaz had told them he was twenty-eight.

When his work at *Sandbostel* was done Clem fled, went AWOL. He had borrowed the army motorbike and given it away to a man outside Dresden.

Fugitives still trudged the banks, not moving their heads left or right; they tramped the tributaries to reach the Elbe itself and cross from Soviet Authority into the British region.

Sometimes he called out to them, "Germans? Where are you from?"

"Yes, Germans – from Brandenburg; from Silesia; from Poland; from Prussia."

They were the ones expelled. The Allies had signed away their land at the stroke of a pen.

A mess of feathers spiked with curved rib bones drifted along beside him for a time; night black feathers slicked with purples and greens.

Some boys slipped like gleaming silver fish from the ledge of a bridge into the water, closing their eyes and mouths against the sewage and rotting flesh and surfaced around a half-submerged barge. They gripped their noses with fingers and rolled under like long-backed tench.

In the bottom of his boat were the remaining tins of spam, milk and dried egg from the motorbike carrier. At the border of the American sector, when he had passed through on the dispatch rider's motorbike before turning east to Dresden, he had seen the Swiss relief lorries turned back. Further on he passed a prisoner of war camp where a German woman had thrown herself in front of the motorbike so that he had to swerve and brake.

"I beg you take this food to my man; they are starving him. He has had no food for many days."

But Clem was turned away from the gates of the camp. Outside the wire fence Clem and the woman watched a soldier set a blazing torch to a pile of wheat.

Beyond Meissen the river took him between the British and the Soviet zone. More refugees had followed rivers that joined the Elbe. Approaching Hamburg still more joined the flow. Some rode carts, their old folk bundled in dusty quilts and grey blankets, their horses slipshod and hoof-sore. Others trailed handcarts, pots and pans roped to their backs like tinkers. The vehicles of the victorious Allies slowed for soldiers to shovel the bodies of the fallen from the road before they could drive on. Flies in swarms hung above the late afternoon river and sucked blood from his neck as the Elbe slid into Hamburg, once port of a thousand tongues.

Slipping into the city Clem scanned the skyline for the ruins of *Hammaburg* Castle, the *Bergedorf* observatory and *Michaeliskirche*. The buildings remaining seemed poised on an invisible edge while all about them laid piles of dust that stirred and caught in the throats of the people leaning into the wind. The boat slipped through broken warehouses, once bursting with grain, now hollow. Single walls here and there stood like sentinels; now and then a complete building was still standing. His oars strained in their metal swivels, their regular creak amplified against the taller of the broken buildings on either side.

He rested, strained arms and back muscles loosening. A reflection of a slice of early moon glimmered in the water, though the sky was awash with light. To his left stood a warehouse several stories high. Clem caught sight of a figure way up on a stone ledge, inching along it. Then more small figures slithered into the building. A wooden shutter flapped.

Children shivering at night, wrapped in Hessian sacks against the chill.

Outside the Fish Auction Hall a crowd gathered. Ruddy fishermen from the villages along the sea and a cluster of barterers with brasses and metal hinges and glass doorknobs for trade. He saw a glint of a silver dish change hands. Fish were cast onto iron casings, found lying about the shipyards, to be steamed in brine. As the fish skins split, people spat out their enmity.

"Hitler should have had his throat slit."

"Where are the Jews, the cause of all this?"

Clem caught sight of Lili in the shadows and Otto, licking fish oil from his lips while Lili waited for her moment.

The next time Clem glanced towards the fire, Lili and Otto were gone. Someone was tolling the curfew on the remaining bells of the city. At dusk the boat reached the confluence with the Alster where a flock of a hundred swans had settled. Surrounding them were the pale faces of a group of men and women holding long rods, an assortment of metal and wood pikes, metal hoops at their ends for catching swans. It took two people to hold each of them as they were dragged to the shore, one clamping the wings closed and the other stretching the swan's neck to break it.

He recognised a woman's face; Lili again, her hair covered with a long headscarf and shoulders with a shawl. "They call this 'The Dead Zone'."

"Where is Otto?" Clem called back. "I could help you." The people on the bank stirred uneasily as though the wind were shivering dead leaves on hard ground.

"Otto is dead," said Lily.

"I should have killed him," said Clem.

"It is not possible. You are Otto. Otto is you."

They shoved the swans into sacks and slung them onto their backs.

Clem made for the District of Altona-North. Landmarks were few. When he came to the place he counted houses down the street. A young woman emerged from the basement steps carrying books. She was thin, wearing a gabardine with the collar turned up. It would have been stylish if it had not been ingrained with dirt. Waves of hair fell about the collar. She walked a few paces over what had been the garden. A series of chimney pots of different sizes lay cracked and tumbled about the fallen masonry.

Clem called out. "Hello."

The young woman shaded her eyes.

"I'm looking for the home of Vogelweide. I am English - with the FAU, Quakers, said Clem."

The young woman didn't speak for a moment and Clem felt he should say more.

"I have some personal possessions to return to the family."

"Vogelweide is my name," she said.

213

"I have some belongings of Otto Vogelweide," said Clem.

"My brother. Yes. I'm Eva Vogelweide"

"I have been given his papers to give you and also this letter. And this box."

She took the letter, then passed it back. "My eyes are not good this afternoon. Would you read it to me?" she asked."

Clem perched on a long dressed stone and began to read.

Dear Eva,

They will tell you I deserted, but that is not so. I was searching for something, not running away; seeking for just one hour free of being a rat swimming over the Kruckau. It is the end. The Reich cannot survive.

Eva, my step sister, like our brother Günther you have impeccable blood. When mine dripped into the dust it was red too. I have lived with a lie so long that I cannot imagine what it would be to live without it — without the lie I turn out to be nothing.

Your loving brother,
Otto.

"Come. Follow me."

Clem followed Eva down a short flight of rough concrete steps into a shelter similar to the Andersons at home. She pulled out the chair from her desk, gestured for Clem to sit down and set an orange crate upright for herself.

"He – Otto, my half brother – would have studied art but the war got in the way. He had terrible rows with my brother Günther. They quarrelled over a woman – Günther's girlfriend, then fiancé, a Jewish girl, Etty Edelmann. Günther and she were at university together when the … the regulations came in. Günther moved from home and hid her in his university flat. It was Otto who gave her away to the authorities."

The lamp cast a sallow light. Above it a low electric light socket dangled bulb-less.

"We have no power," she said, tracing the direction of his gaze. "I'll brew nettle tea presently."

She went over to a shelf and pulled out a book. Behind it was a pouch. She opened it and began rolling a cigarette, using only a few strings of tobacco fibres. She made a second one and handed it to Clem. Clem accepted. He would give her a gift of tobacco before he left. He rooted to find matches. The match flared brightly in the underground bunker. He lit hers and then his own.

Looking round he made out that the place was lined with books. Plans or maps were pinned to the shelves themselves and a table was set up in the middle. He peered at one of the plans, tracing the Alster into its basins, the Außenalster and the Binnenalster.

"I'm piecing together who lived where and who has returned." She glanced at a half-drawn plan pinned to a shelf. "This is our old neighbourhood. We were given the house where a Jewish family had lived when ours was bombed. Recently it has been taken over by the military government as a food distribution centre. So I returned here to our old house - at least here I live in my own grave."

Clem tapped his cigarette on the edge of a saucer. "I have an interest in maps myself."

"Many historical plans of the city have been lost. We lost two thirds of the books from the town library in the bombing" She leaned forward, planting her elbows on her knees, "I write letters, try to make contact with someone of influence in the Military Government. I have been working with the former communist resistance. However we are ignored."

Clem blew a smoke ring that thinned gradually. "I would like you to meet a friend of mine... Lili... if we can find her. I believe she may have returned. She used to live around here somewhere."

They saw the cart of turnips and potatoes first. For these Lili had traded two lace collars from the bundle her mother had bricked up in the cellar. She had bartered at one of the farms out in the *Waldorfer*.

"I inhabit the part of the house that still stands. A woman spat on me and shouted, 'Coming back for your money, Jew?'".

Later she said, "I want to be sure you understand. *I killed your brother*, Eva."

Eva yanked at silverweed growing by the bridge where they stood, but it gripped the ground with a deep tap root.

"Did you ever read Grimm's fairy tales? My people let ourselves be put under enchantment. Now we are imprisoned as ravens in a glass mountain," she said. She straightened up slowly. "He is better dead. My father killed his spirit long ago. Now my father is incarcerated in *Neuengamme*; the concentration camp of the Nazis is the prison camp of the new authority." She put her arm around Lili and kissed her, "How could I be bitter towards you? But we'll fight here by the *Trostbruke;* we'll fight for new life; we'll fight so that we remember; so that we do not forget."

Eva was strong, though she looked like a branch of sallow by a pond. Lili fought like a rearing horse. Afterwards they embraced, hugging each other tight like mother and daughter.

"Look," said Eva, as she examined a fungus growing by the roots of a birch tree. "Yellow birch boletus. The roots are alive even though the tree seems dead. New growth might still break out.

"Hamburg was always anti-Nazi." she continued, "We spent our nights in Bramfeld out in the woods after the air raids. There was talk that the Nazis were finished. Günther told me he must go into the heart of the furnace after Otto betrayed him.

Lili laid her hand gently over Eva's.

217

."Because of their child. She was three months pregnant when she went to Auschwitz."

"She gave birth. Afterwards, we were told, he was shot as he jumped from the gatehouse. The baby was hidden in the front of his jacket. She was crushed. Someone sent me two diaries. Etty wrote that she had given the child the name, Mirrie."

A circle of musicians played a tabor drum and pipe. The drum was slung on a leather strap under Dirk's arm and he beat it with a short bone flicked by one wrist; broad, flat fingers stopping the pipe with the other. There were two fiddles, a melodeon and a concertina, several pipes, recorders and whistles and a set of bagpipes. The dancers formed in two lines facing each other, their arms linked, as though propping each other upright. They danced as though their lives depended on it. Lili's long dark hair was loose and she wore a soot-smeared red beret pulled over her ears. She was supported by a man on either side but sank lower and lower. Her jaw dropped and her head rolled. For a while the dancers dragged her back and forth, though her body slumped.

"Stop! Stop!" Clem shouted.

He took a few steps forward. One of the men holding her released her arm and she dangled from the other man until he also let go. The men linked arms staring ahead of them into the dark.

Eva rushed forward and dragged the corpse away by the heels, her head knocking against stones. Clem took Lili's body under the arms and together they made toward the blaze, the corpse swinging between them

"*The Silken Knot.*" bellowed a fiddler behind them and the music broke over them again. The emaciated body hung momentarily over the flames above the glowing tinder. Her body would rest on the cinders of others.

The fiddler cried, "*The Wounded Hussar*," and the music slowed. The dancers took longer strides raising their arms, each one's knuckles knotted to the next ones.

The flow of the swelling Elbe vibrated Raven against a barricade of old oil cans and wooden spars. She might be suspended in forgetfulness until this river ran dry. Distantly she became aware of the voices of two men as they examined her carcass. She flexed her claw experimentally.

"If it wasn't for the filth of this place it would be almost worth pulling it out and having a look to see how freshly dead it was," said one.

"What kind of a bird is it anyway? I've never seen anything like that size before." said the other.

Raven's temper ignited. She signalled to her torn musculature and began to rejoin fragments of bone. She slotted her vertebrae back like a jigsaw, rethreaded her wing pins and stretched elastic over the frame.

219

July

Lou

The air thrummed with heat. They had constructed boats of dried umbellifer stems, of pignut and angelica, with masts and outriggers of reedy grasses for balance. Clem said that his mother used to bring him to this deep cleft of the West Allen as a child and Lou liked the idea of things coming full circle.

"Come on, they're ready," she called. "Let's launch them both at the same moment."

They balanced on bare feet across the river's flood beach. It gushed deep brown through this rift, its bed of glacial stones and boulders narrowing to a triangular groove as it forced its way through a fault. They let the boats idle in a little bay, where they rotated aimlessly for a while. Then Lou's boat caught on the lip of the little inlet and spun out, almost keeling over with the force. Clem tapped his to send it straight into the main surge.

"You cheat," laughed Lou.

Clem's boat too swirled and half sank. Lou's careered into a rock further down and stayed there, trapped. She sprang up and shuffled off her yellow skirt. Underneath she wore her black and white striped bathing costume. She dipped her toe into the water and drew back, shocked by the chill, but steeled herself to paddle into the shallows. Clem left his trousers on the bank and tested the water with his toes. The bed shelved so that by the time Lou reached the rock the water had risen to her waist. One by one Lou released the twigs and leaves that had caught behind the rock. Clem waded up behind and caught her lightly round the waist. She turned to face him. His eye lashes were covered in droplets of water.

"I don't know why my mother entrusted me to you," she smiled.

He pulled her very gently closer and then she slipped through his arms and swam free until she reached a flat rock and pulled herself out. Clem scrambled through the gap beneath her rock following in the wake of the boats

"Come on," he called.

Further on the water fell into an eely pool in a bell pit of rock, a bowl enclosing the pool on three sides. A waterfall roared above, misting the air with water droplets. Lou paused before venturing in, but Clem took her hand and led her from the shallows, tugging her deeper. Under the waterfall they couldn't hear themselves. Clem ducked and rose on the other side of the fall and mouthed the words.

"I love you."

She mouthed the same words back to him.

Then he mouthed something else, very slowly.

"Will you marry me?"

And she took the plunge

He lifted his arms in the air and yelled. And the war seemed far away...

...as they scrambled in their gabardines and waded ankle deep through waves lapping with debris at the edge of the sea; old tins of Bird's custard, cartridge and grenade cases.

"Sometimes I think people are like oysters" said Lou. "They form a hard shell over their fear so you can't trust them to know what is true. You have to go into the world and decide for yourself. Do you know who I suddenly thought of today? Etty Edelman, who once gave me a piece of amber in exchange for my best story and then told her best story all the same. It was before the war when we had some German girls to stay at the Colony for the International Peace Exchange. People of different faiths came to learn about each other. I must have been about eight.

She paused and scanned the shore. "Everyone liked Etty because she knew lots of ghost stories."

Further out the samphire collectors with their flat willow baskets and trousers and skirts tucked up were bobbing like wagtails as they picked. They would steep the plump green fingers in vinegar and bottle them to sell on their whelk and eel stalls.

"Do you think they can indoctrinate you to hate a friend because of her race or creed, as easily as you can be taught to understand her?" she asked.

"You would have to believe that she had done something really wrong and broken your trust. But then you'd have to trust your teacher when she tried to change your original belief," Fern replied.

"And people aren't to be believed any more. There's a time when you think grown-ups must be right, but those days are over now."

The samphire collectors moved on towards the sand spit where a dead tree was still rooted, the remnant of an older shoreline.

"I wonder where she is now, Etty Edelman," finished Lou.

Clem

The Lych gate had a wooden seat on either side. They could hear the hubbub of the wedding as a hum from the other side of the church.

"Escaped," said Clem.

"Its a little bit like hiding in the bike sheds before school," said Lou.

The soft breathy call of pigeons blew from above. A foot-crunch on the gravel made them both look up. The young man was slender with a coarse mop of highland-cattle hair. His eyes were crinkled in the dark hollows of his eye sockets.

He stepped forward and held out his hands, "Clem."

Clem was back in Hamburg. "Dirk. The drummer. How good to see you. Look at you. So tall and mature." The two embraced. "Dirk this is my new wife Lou. Lou, darling, this is my good friend Dirk from Germany."

Lou took Dirk's proffered hand, "I'm so pleased to meet you Dirk. I know so little of Clem's former life."

"Clem found me... in a grocery store. He rescued my brother, Felix, and I. Weaned me off a gun - and onto drumsticks instead. We survived because he got us into the Quaker orphanage. Anyway I'm at University in New York now."

"I don't pretend to understand, except that it sounds as though he did what he could," said Lou.

Dirk nodded.

"And you're still playing the drums?" asked Clem.

"Yes – at first I gave up... after Lili. But Eva persuaded me to 'keep our story alive in the rhythm of the drums'. Oh and she gave me something for you Clem."

Dirk held out a brown paper package. Inside was a copy of *Grimm's Fairy Tales*.

"She sent you a message – 'from beyond the grave' she said. She died a few months after Lili in the freeze of the winter of '47."

The flyleaf was inscribed in a shaky cursive script.

'Although we don't own it, the smallest of tales keeps us alive. When the time is right I know you will tell our stories.'

Clem didn't speak. Lou took his hand and Dirk's and they held on to each other.

Raven

At timetabled intervals dust rose from the shelves of the Literary and Philosophical Library. The books and their contents shuddered with the vibrations of steam trains entering and leaving the station. Clem chewed over volumes of *Haklyuts Voyages* with their tales of early exploration and plantation in Virginia.

When the day of the Tribunal arrived he sat downstairs and scribbled on a sheet of paper, crossing bits out and writing them over and over, filling the margins and annotating above the title and between the lines. He did not at first notice the old woman with pearl-white hair, streaked with a purple gloss, who bent her head over a book in the end bay.

"Grandma? What are you doing here?"

"What does it look like, child?"

"But you can't read."

"Now, that's where you're wrong. The book of life is illuminated for all who choose to look."

He had no time to think about what she might mean. From far above there was a clang like a massive iron bar dropping onto a metal platform. As the blocks of flooring cracked along the lines of the herringbone pattern and the books began to tremble on their shelves the two leapt from their seats and clutched each other's hands. A sapling of ash thrust through the floor, shattering it into a mosaic of crazed pieces.

Of course it had been an accident waiting to happen, they said later. The Victorian drainage system needed a complete overhaul; besides which the Library had been built into cellars of mediaeval houses, shaken by trains arriving and leaving over so many years. The readers took refuge in the station. A muscular young man sprang from the foot plate of a train and sped along the platform to fetch a trolley.

"Quickly" he called, "we haven't long." His ginger hair flopped over one eye.

"I've not finished sorting all of the shoes from the last delivery. I sorted colours and male and female," Leo said apologetically.

He steered the trolley between others who were already unloading and sorting shoes from carriages further up the train. A heap of shoes tumbled out and Leo grabbed a barrow and loaded up the spilling contents. Clem snatched a shovel from the platform and climbed into the van, working from the inside. He picked up a pair of leather lace ups knotted together, worn the colour of conkers; then a pair of pointed-toed silk shoes in faded bronze with a tiny heel.

"Where is this train from?" he asked

"Oh this is an express straight out of Central Europe," replied Leo. "But I can't stop and talk. Come on."

Clem glanced at his watch uneasily. He would be late, but it would be churlish to refuse. Another barrow had been left standing on the platform. He filled it and followed as Leo wheeled his own barrow out of the station and began pushing it up the cobbled hill on the other side.

To his right Clem glimpsed the Literary and Philosophical Library where the Tribunal was to meet. It looked solid enough. The *Bigg Market* was deserted. Clem caught a glimpse of the burn as it slithered under the Low Bridge and thought how odd it was that it should be exposed after Dobson and Grainger had hidden it under the street. They turned into a street he didn't recognise; half-timbered houses provided a little shelter from the snow where the upper storey jutted out.

His barrow weighed increasingly on his arms and he began to think perhaps this was an impossible task. How were they to know who the shoes belonged to? Leo moved on purposefully and Clem realised that they were in a market. Snow began to fall. They set their barrows down and people gathered to look.

"Why is everyone in such a hurry?" Clem asked.

"It is nearly time for the curfew," said a stall holder. "In the ghetto, you must take care not to be out after the nine o clock bell."

A fiddle player bowed the strings of her instrument. Clem looked up and saw a young woman digging into a pile of boots. She felt into the toe of each pair until she produced a crumpled piece of paper from a wrinkled right foot and made off with both boots and paper.

Clem shouted, "Stop her."

Etty turned her head at the sound of his voice.

"No. No," said the stall-holder and Clem recognised Reuben's face peering anxiously at him. "There is no payment. These souls have already paid."

Clem glanced at his father's pocket watch. The Tribunal would already be in session. Would he find his way back from here? He caught sight of the pinnacled tower of St. Nicholas' Cathedral and hurried towards lower-lying land until he found himself outside the library. The white door stood open. He stood for a moment staring at the black beading outlining each panel.

Inside he climbed the wrought iron steps to the gallery and made for the meeting room. The lawyer was in full flow. He recognised the bishop, his tutor from university and, of course, his father.

"You're late" whispered Ephraim. "They asked me at my Tribunal what I would do if an enemy soldier raped my sister. What I could not tell him was that violence did not belong to the enemy. We must remove violence from ourselves."

When his turn came, Clem felt that he was expected to play a part on stage but had forgotten to learn the lines. His father made excuses for his speechlessness.

At the station he heard the groan of brakes and the howling whistle. The train was windowless and towered above him. It halted and doors were flung open. People buzzed around a carriage near the tender. A whoosh of flame scorched his hair as it belched from a narrow ventilation slit.

A woman's voice shouted, "We'll have to board her."

A chain of people passed fire buckets filled with sand to an official in thick gloves who had wrestled the door open despite the red hot handles. Flames shot out in a flare of oxygen. Lili got there before him and grasped burning books by the armful. She grimaced. As she handed them over, another woman doused them. Someone had lit charcoal braziers. Clem held the books' pages to dry. It seemed a hopeless task. One book fell open at the dedication: *'to Etty to celebrate the day of your birth. With love from Mama and Papa, 19th November 1918.'* Another dropped to the floor, open at a view of Prague from beyond the town walls, a drawing by Wenceslas Hollar. Clem marked the page with a scrap of half charred paper and slipped the book into his jacket pocket.

"It's my Tribunal this afternoon," he told Lili, shamefaced.

He watched as barrows crammed with books were wheeled into one of the *Lit. and Phil's* underground rooms. There was a touch on his shoulder and he turned to confront his father.

"What are you doing here? You were permitted only a few moments for a breath of air. Quickly; we'll climb back to the gallery by the spiral stairs."

"I'm just…"

"They're all waiting for you. Don't let me down after all I've done for you. You are my *only* son." His father began to cry.

The empty seat at the oval table was still warm.

"Which would you rather do – build a bridge or mend a man's arm?" asked the engineer.

"The two are interdependent," he said. "A bridge can be a structure that joins two sides of a ravine or a way for one person to touch another. If a bridge is broken, it can only be mended with the goodwill of the people on both sides of the river."

A Mission band was playing in the station. A stream of people pushing barrows flowed towards the river. They flooded over the High Level Bridge towards the glass factory. In their barrows were heaped hundreds of pairs of spectacles. "Where are we going?" he called to a hurrying woman. She slowed and joined him. He recognized Eva's bright eyes.

"Didn't you know?" she said. "All the shattered glass of Europe comes here to be melted down and made into…"

Her voice dropped and a wisp of hair blew across her face. She drew slightly closer and he smelled decaying stomach contents on her breath. "They say they are building a glass mountain, topped with a palace of ice."

"So that they can see our thoughts?"

"You're the architect," she said, "You tell me."

A young man slid open a matchbox. "I heard that it would be a museum, its collection of exhibits to represent all we have made," he said.

The people directing the barrows were robed as priests and bishops. "Whose are these spectacles?" he asked a woman who was cradling a child in a bundle of rags. He recognised Etty again.

"Sometimes it is spectacles sometimes it is the glass fronts of pocket watches," she said. "It is different every night. We never know what they are going to bring in next. We are made to sort through them, shelve and label them."

Etty lowered herself onto a stone stool in the aisle, took her breast from the folds of her dress and held her hand behind the child's head. As Clem watched, her breast began to shrivel until it drooped to a limp, small sack. The baby cried, unable to suck.

"Is there a woman here with a drop of milk to spare?" he shouted.

There was silence as if a child had brought up a shameful matter at the dinner table. The priests glared at him.

"We must all conserve what we've got for our families," another woman shouted.

He flew upwards. Across the river he could see St Mary's church on one side and All Saints on the other. There were the cupola and spires of St. Nicholas. The river gleamed, teeming with keel boats, coal barges, tugs and warships.

The sky darkened as he looked west towards the sunset behind the bridges; at the High level pumping sparking trains, a vein of fire; at the station curved like a caterpillar and now at the dome on the top of the *Lit. and Phil. Library*, its glass windows ajar. He slid in, knocking books tumbling like the stones of the city that would tremble and break apart. He stood in the doorway of the Meeting Room as several heads turned and the chairman shuffled his papers.

A throat was cleared. "Ah. Mr Renshaw. We have one or two more questions to put to you."

He knew the voice.

Clem slipped into the seat reserved for him.

Straight away the City Engineer – he hadn't recognized Otto before – fired a question. "Would you kill to protect your mother? Would you kill your brother if he were about to murder your mother?"

"Could I trade my life for another's? Can anyone know before that moment arrives?"

"Let's try another angle; Adolph Hitler also studied architecture."

"We cannot blame the science of architecture for the human motives that underlie the design of a death camp."

His tutor, Dr Günther Vogelweide leaned forward. "How do you know you are a pacifist?" he asked.

"Every human being from both the victorious and vanquished parties is a victim of war. No-one who has been made to wage war on another, by overt or covert means, can avoid being brutalised by the experience."

Günther leaned back in his chair and stroked his chin thoughtfully. "

Auguste Vogelweide took a gulp of water.

"Is it not human nature to do violence? We are of the animal kingdom after all."

"If one of us has been driven to do something, any of us can do it. War can bring out the bad nature in those who fight it rather than the good nature."

Vogelweide shuffled uncomfortably on the hard ladder-backed chair. Beads of sweat broke out on Clem's forehead.

"Is not respect for your father the greatest good?" asked Vogelweide.

"I thought I had killed my brother by becoming a pacifist. I thought I had killed my father by not being a good enough pacifist. But now I know that while I live I *am* my brother and I *am* my father. "

"That sounds like sophistry to me." said Otto. "What would happen if everyone refused to fight? Then what?"

"If I am trapped in a history that is unpalatable then it is up to me to know that it is my own history and speak it."

Günther nodded thoughtfully, "No more *sprachregelung?* Only words that mean what they say?"

Then they were whispering.

"He wants to save his soul."

"He thinks words will save him."

Günther began to laugh. Then the others joined in until their laughter spiralled hysterically.

He tried to speak, but it was not possible. The words from Etty's diary rang in his mind, the reason why he must be a pacifist and why he feared to be a pacifist: *I, too, am Otto.*

"I'm sorry. I'm afraid I have no story to tell…"

At the door of the meeting room a figure in a dark feathered cloak, a swathe of white hair falling down her back, swept spilled shoes into a sack.

Was it a white door with black beading that swung open and slammed shut leaving him stranded on the other side?

August

Lou

"Do you think life goes on after you lose someone you love, Fern?"

"Some things don't. But you have your memories. And life itself does. You father was a lovely man. One of the best."

"It worries me packing to leave so soon afterwards, leaving Mother. I am doing the right thing aren't I, Fern? Going to the frozen wastes of the North East."

"You have your sleigh and furs and your warm-hearted lover."

"Shall I take this? I can't decide whether it's past life or future." She held up the greatcoat she had worn during the war. "Part of me wants to leave it behind – but it still fits. It never seems to wear out. Only it's getting a bit thin on the cuffs. I'm leaving the last of my childhood books and jigsaws behind for the rag and bone and the jumble.

"Take the coat. It'll keep the Siberian winds at bay. It was a jolly good thing you both landing jobs in the same school."

"I know. Very different this time though. No Barnado's class, but Clem says they are Anglo Saxons in Seahouses. And they speak their mind."

"You'll do fine," said Fern.

Lou pressed down the clothes in the tan leather case and snapped it closed. She sat on the bed and reached into the bedside table drawer, fished about and grasped the stone.

"Look what I found when I was sorting things out."

"Amber," said Fern.

"It belonged to Etty, the girl from the Peace Camp years ago, who told me the story of Raven the Creator. I'll pass on her chunk of amber in exchange for your best story."

Fern held the amber up to the light. "I'll pass it on to Robin one day, but for now I *do* have one more story," she said.

Once there was a woman who travelled with her prince into a distant kingdom. Now this prince was under an enchantment and part of him was sleeping. He took her to live under a glass mountain where his memories dwelt. Every night the woman collected wood and built a fire and when it was roaring she took her prince's hands and warmed them by it and with her kisses she warmed his heart. Until one day the deep part of him awoke and all was well.

A Note on Sources

A great deal of reading and listening has influenced my own telling and interpretation of oral tales re-worked in this book. I am grateful to the tellers of traditional tales, particularly to Manu Tupou *Raven: Creator of the World's Eskimo Legends* Caedmon Cassette CDL 51422; Sheila Douglas (1987) *The King of the Black Art and other folk tales,* Aberdeen University Press; Bill Reid (1984) *The Raven Steals the Light,* Douglas and McIntyre and The University of Washington Press; Betty Rosen (1991) *Shapers and Polishers: Teachers as Storytellers,* Collins Educational.

My understanding of the contemporary study of architecture and the art of architecture was assisted by my reading of the following works, to which reference is also made in the text. A. E. Richardson and Hector O. Corfiato (1938) *The Art of Architecture* London: The English Universities Press Ltd; tochvil (1965) *Hollar's Journey on the Rhine* (R.F. Samsour, Trans.) Prague: Artia; J.M. Dent & Sons (1913-14) *Everyman's Encyclopaedia* (3rd ed. 1949-50) London: Author.

Other books which were valuable in gaining an insight into the themes of the book included: Lyn Smith (1998) *Pacifists in Action: The Experience of the Friend's Ambulance Unit in the Second World War,* York: Sessions of York; Roger Bush (1998) *FAU: The Third Generation: Friends Ambulance Unit Post-War Service 1946-9* York: Sessions of York; Tzvetan Todorov (1991) *Facing the Extreme: Moral Life in the Concentration Camps* London: Weidenfeld and Nicolson; James Baque (1997) *Crimes and Mercies: The Fate of German Civilians under Allied Occupation 1944-1950* London: Time Warner; Hans A. Schmitt (1997) *Quakers and Nazis: Innner Light in Outer Darkness* Missouri: University of Missouri Press; Robert Graves and Raphael Patai (1983) *Hebrew Myths: The Book of Genesis* New York: Greenwich House; Raphael Patai (1967) *The Hebrew Goddess* (3rd Ed.) Detroit: Wayne State University Press, 1990; Evelyn Wilcock (1994) *Pacifism and the Jews* Stroud: Hawthorn Press.

The Yeats poem alluded to on page 94 is W.B. Yeats (1899) 'The Song of Wandering Aengus' from *The Wind Among the Reeds.*